CHRISTMAS AT PELICAN BEACH

PELICAN BEACH BOOK FOUR

MICHELE GILCREST

D1506304

GET A FREE EBOOK!

Would you like a FREE book? JOIN Michele's newsletter to receive information about new releases, giveaways, and special promotions! To say thank you, I'll send you a FREE copy of The Inn at Pelican Beach. Sign up today!

https://dl.bookfunnel.com/wr9wvokoin

JOLENE

*M*ost of the family knew me as Cousin Jolene. I'm a southerner born and raised in Jacksonville, Florida. They describe me as a bit of a hell-raiser, but mainly when somebody makes me cross. For the most part, I'm still very well respected. Occasionally, I let my tongue get the best of me. It's probably my 'no filter' approach that gets me into trouble. I'm not the beating around the bush type. Never have been and never will. Most say I'm nontraditional because I naturally go against the grain. Overall, I'd like to think I have good intensions behind everything I do.

About five months ago my cousin's wife, Helen, reached out and asked me to move to Pelican Beach. She said she needed help with taking care of Cousin Will. His dementia had settled in and changed their lives tremendously. Helen wanted to ensure that Will received round-the-clock care. With my former background as a nurse, I didn't mind helping. I spent far too many Christmases alone with memories of my late husband

and a bottle of something to soothe the pain. This year I planned to do differently.

I spent most of my days helping Will get dressed, cooking his meals, and making sure he maintained a routine schedule. We were fast approaching the Christmas holiday, and even if Will's daughters weren't thrilled about my presence, at least for now, I was here to stay.

"He's making a list..." I sang and shimmied around the staircase while wrapping it with garland. My eggnog was spiked with a special concoction that was sure to help me relax. It was my reward after a hard day's work.

"Jolene, what in the world are you into now?" Helen stood, looking all righteous with her hand on her hip. Lately, it seemed like she had a lot to say about the way I spent my free time. Honestly, she had a lot to say about everything.

"Oh, loosen up, Helen. You should pour yourself a glass. When you're done, come join me in caroling and decorating. This place could use a little sprucing up."

"I'm happy to decorate with you, but I'll pass on whatever it is you're drinking," she said.

"That's your problem. You need to learn how to relive your glory days and let your hair down and have a good time. Now, pass me the lights so I can wrap them around the garland."

The taste of brandy and eggnog soothed my palate and helped ease some tension. I continued to hum along while stacking a few pine cones in a glass vase near the fireplace.

"It's hard to think about having a good time when there's so much that needs to be done, Jolene. I'm so far behind this year. Normally I'd have the entire house decorated by Thanksgiving." She sifted through the boxes, looking for another string of lights.

"You know what they say... better late than never!"

"I guess."

"Santa baby....da da daaa." The sound of the front door creaking open caught me by surprise. Rebecca walked in and completely killed my buzz. She was Will and Helen's youngest daughter, and she wasn't very fond of me.

"Hi, Mom." She kissed Helen and then looked over my way. "Cousin Jolene."

"Rebecca, it's too mild in Pelican Beach for you to come in here with such a frosty attitude. Why don't you hand over that sweet baby of yours and grab some decorations. We need to help your mother get this cottage ready for Christmas."

She reluctantly handed John William over.

"There he is. What a handsome boy," I said as I nuzzled my nose against his.

"It smells like cinnamon and nutmeg in here, Mom. What are you cooking?"

"Jolene baked a batch of cinnamon rolls this afternoon. Maybe that's what you smell, dear. Help yourself if you want one."

"Santa baby...la la de dum." I danced around the living room with John William to keep up with the music in the background.

"Jolene, have you been drinking?" Rebecca asked.

"That's Cousin Jolene, to you. A little eggnog hurt nobody."

"It's not the eggnog that I'm worried about. It's what you put in it." She scooped John William out of my arms.

"Come to momma. It's time for your nap, sweet boy."

"I've been trying to tell Jolene she needs to lighten up with all the drinking, but she doesn't listen to me." Helen widened her eyes from the top of the staircase and frowned at me.

"Okay, Helen. Let's have this conversation once and for all. I'm in here minding my business, not bothering a soul. If I want to have a nightcap, I don't see any harm in it. So what's the real issue? I work hard day and night to help with Will. But you're always taking issue with something. Whatever happened to you? Since when did you become such a goody two shoes?"

"Pardon me, Jolene."

"Ohhhh, here we go. 'Pardon me, Jolene... pardon me.' Who are you? I didn't realize how much you've changed over the years. You must've forgotten that I knew you from way back when. You know, the Helen who used to party and have a good time. You used to shimmy for Will and a few of your other lovers back then. And, that was as a married woman! I'd hate for everybody to know what you were like when you were single."

Rebecca's mouth dropped.

"Jolene, that's enough! You've had way too much to drink tonight and I won't stand here and listen to another word. Rebecca and I can finish the decorations. Why don't you head upstairs and sleep it off," Helen said with a flushed look on her face.

"Oh, when I tell the truth now you want to call it a night. I guess your precious little angels don't know about your hay days in Savannah. If Uncle Samuel was still alive, I bet he'd have a lot to say about your visits. Him and his neighbors!"

"Jolene, I'm warning you!"

"What was that guy's name again? You know, the one who lived across the street?"

"Jolene Ferguson, that's enough!" Helen yelled.

The room fell silent except for the Christmas music still playing in the background.

"Well, now you know how it feels. The constant remarks... the judgement. Jolene this... and Jolene that."

Helen and Rebecca were just as silent as could be.

"Well, anyway. Helen... if you want to hold on to secrets and walk around here acting all high and mighty, it's fine by me... that's your business. Just leave me out of it! Remember, you're the one that called me here. Not the other way around."

"Mom, are you just going to stand there and take this from her?"

"Rebecca, stay out of it." Helen sounded cross as she began tossing a few of the decorations back in the boxes.

"She's not letting me get away with anything. I'm just telling it like it is."

William slowly shuffled into the room and stopped to look at everyone.

"What's all the racket out here?" He stood in his striped pajamas with a disgruntled look on his face. He was probably aggravated that his rest was being interrupted more than anything else.

"It's just us girls getting way too excited about Christmas decorations. Come on, Will. Let me take you back to your room so you can stretch your legs and get comfortable."

I took Will by the arm and caught a glimpse of Helen's misty eyes and Rebecca walking over to console her.

It was just past midnight, and I was having trouble falling to sleep. I sat in the kitchen staring out the window at the moonlight with a glass in hand. The sound of bedroom slippers approaching from behind let me know that I wasn't alone.

"Don't worry, Helen. I'm just sitting here drinking a glass of water, that's all."

I didn't have to look behind me to know it was her. In my short time living here, I'd mastered the sound of everyone's footsteps in the late night hour.

"I wasn't going to say a word. I don't think I have enough energy to engage in another round with you, Jolene."

I continued to stare outside while noticing her profile in my peripheral.

"About that. I suppose I owe you an apology. While I haven't been too fond of your comments as of late, I could've handled it differently."

"You were harsh, but I guess I had it coming. Besides, it's no secret that you can be a pistol when you want to be."

We both chuckled.

"Yep, Jolene Pistol Ferguson. That's me." My new nickname had a ring to it and left me with a lingering smile.

"Why don't you pull up a chair and stay for a while."

Helen pulled out one of the chairs at the table and sat a few feet away.

"Look. I've been sitting here trying to figure this whole thing out. I don't know how to sugarcoat things, so I'm going to give it to you straight, Helen. In order for this arrangement to continue to work, I need to be treated like an adult. I've endured five long months filled with your passive comments and suggestions about how I ought to do things. Hell, I'm surprised I lasted this long. It almost feels like my late mother has risen from the dead. She had a way with bossing me around in my adult years. It ain't gonna fly with me, Helen. That's not who I am, and you knew this before you asked me to come stay with you."

"I guess that makes two of us with an axe to grind. I worry about you, Jolene. But not so much that I'm going to let you turn my house upside down. This is the most I've ever seen you drink and carry on the way you do. When you're sober, you're fine. But when you're drinking, I don't know who needs more looking after, Will or you. More importantly, I refuse to allow you to ruin my Christmas. Arguing with me and drudging up the past in front of my family will not be tolerated. I won't say one more thing about the way you live your life as long as I'm treated with decency and respect underneath my roof."

I kept my voice low as not to wake up Will. This wouldn't be the first time Helen and I had a little spat, and I'm sure it wouldn't be the last.

"Fine. I'll limit my recreational time to the evening once I've settled in my room. As long as you can agree to keeping your comments to yourself and treating me like I'm an adult."

"Deal." Helen extended her hand across the table.

"Deal!" I swatted her hand out of the way in a jovial manner. "Get out of here with all the handshaking. What would a real family be without a healthy spat every now and again?"

"If you say so, Jolene. You aimed below the belt this time and you know it."

"I may have, but you were plucking my last nerve, Helen. How long have I been here now? You never once stopped to ask me how I'm doing, or how I'm settling in to my new life here at the beach. Shoot, I need to have a drink at least once a day to help get over the fact that I left my life behind in Jacksonville."

"Well, Jolene, we never said this was indefinite. If you're not happy, why didn't you say something?"

"It's not that. I just need someone to care about me, that's all. I've spent the last several Christmases alone, in the home that George and I built a life in. I was drowning in debt... my life was a mess. When you called and this opportunity came along, I thought it would be a fresh start. A chance to feel vibrant and live again."

"I don't know how vibrant you expected to feel while caring for a seventy-five-year-old, but okay... I'm listening."

"You get what I'm trying to say. Clearly I'm here to help, but I don't work twenty-four seven. I'm in a new place with lots to see and people to meet. It's a fresh start, Helen. And, though I'm getting older, I'm tired of hanging my head in my sorrows. I just want to let my hair down and be happy again."

"I want that for you," she said.

"You do?"

"Yes. Just as long as it doesn't involve starting a war with the family this Christmas, I'm all for it."

I cocked my head back and laughed so hard.

"Pardon me, Helen. Pardon me!" I continued to chuckle.

Now, this was the Helen I knew coming up as young women. We never allowed a pink elephant to take up residence in our space. We knew how to hash things out but also laugh and have a good time. And the one thing we shared in common was our love for Cousin Will.

PAYTON

I sat in the dining area at the inn waiting for my sisters to arrive. This was my first time inside the inn since my parents sold it. I didn't know what to expect, but the old place had charm and was rather inviting. Some guests were dining by candlelight with heating lamps on the veranda. Others were stopping by the grand Christmas tree in the main foyer to admire its beauty. One by one, as guests arrived, they received Christmas cookies by the concierge. The entire scene looked like something straight out of a holiday movie.

Abby and I agreed to meet Rebecca here for dinner. She said something about it being a pressing matter, but knowing her, she was just probably being dramatic. Now that her baby was getting older and things were back into full swing at her law firm, I'm surprised she had additional time to spare. As for me, I was just looking forward to an evening out with my sisters that included a nice meal and a glass of wine.

Abby's life seemed just as hectic, but for different reasons.

She was a busy stay at home mom who took on way too many extra-curricular responsibilities. If she wasn't hosting PTA events, then she was always loading the kids up in their SUV going somewhere. Every time we spoke they were heading to soccer practice for Aiden or ballet for Maggie. Whenever she complained I just listened. She wasn't fooling anybody with all the fussing. We all knew she loved being there for the kids.

"Well, look what the cat dragged in. I can't believe what I'm seeing. Both of my sisters are here on time."

"It's a miracle I made it at all. Ethan almost got called into a meeting which would've left baby John and I stranded." Rebecca pulled her chair up and signaled for a server.

"I barely made it on time myself," Abby said. "It seems like Wyatt doesn't know how to function unless I set everything up for the kids before I leave. All he had to do was take the dinner out of the fridge and heat it up. Is that too much to ask? How much do you want to bet when I get back no one will have taken a bath or be in bed."

"I don't know how you two do it. I'm exhausted just listening to you."

Thankfully, Cole and I didn't have the same struggles. Maybe it was because I married into a ready-made family, I'm not really sure. But Emmie was in middle school and very independent. The only thing we had to stay on top of was coordinating our schedules.

"Is it just me or does this place look amazing?" Abby was checking out the decor.

"I mean... they have it lit up in here like a Christmas broadway spectacular, but I like it. It's vibrant!" she said.

"Meh. It's alright. I could take it or leave it," Rebecca responded.

After the server took our orders, I shifted my attention toward Rebecca.

"Alright, we've been in suspense long enough. Let's have it. What's this pressing family matter that you texted us about?"

"I don't even know where to begin. Last night I stopped by Mom and Dad's to check on them real quick before heading home. I swear I can't remember the last time I had a normal house visit with them since Jolene arrived."

"That makes two of us," Abby said.

"Jolene was drinking as usual. Wait, I stand corrected. It's not Jolene...it's Cousin Jolene as she ever so politely reminded me. I mean, how dare I call her by her name."

"Alright, Rebecca, get to the point." I couldn't stand all the buildup. It was putting me on edge.

"Anyway, Jolene said a few things that really struck a nerve with Mom. I mean really struck a nerve!"

"Like what?" Abby asked.

"Mom was getting on her case about drinking too much. Jolene retorted by telling Mom that she needed to relax. She recalled how Mom used to know how to have a good time back in the day. She even mentioned something about Mom having a good time with Dad and her other lovers in their early days of being married."

"What? That's ridiculous. It was probably just the liquor talking." I knew our mother better than that. This sounded like a bunch of nonsense. Especially coming from Jolene.

"That's what I thought at first, but it gets worse. Jolene then went on to say, 'I guess your precious little angels don't know about your hay days in Savannah. If Uncle Samuel was still alive I bet he'd have a whole lot to say about your visits to Savannah. Him and his neighbors!' Then she said, 'What was that guy's name again? You know, the one who lived across the street?' I mean, even if she did have too much to drink she shared a lot of details if you ask me! And, the only thing Mom was doing was sitting there and taking it."

Abby looked annoyed. "You didn't speak up for her?" she asked.

"What was I supposed to say? Mom told me to hush and stay out of it. Besides, it didn't look like she was denying one word of it. It kind of got me to thinking about the night of Dad's seventy-fifth birthday party. You remember when we were all standing around in the kitchen and Payton was telling us about Susan cheating on her husband? Mom was the only one defending her and trying to protect her privacy. She kept talking about how we shouldn't judge Susan, and nobody is perfect, and so on, and so forth."

"Oh yeah, that was the night Mom slipped and admitted that she knew the guilt associated with stepping outside of a marriage. I was always curious to know more of the details, but never wanted to push it. You know Mom came up during a time where it was taboo to talk about such things," Abby said.

"Exactly. Haven't you ever wondered more about that situation? Nobody questioned her any further, but it has always lingered in the back of my mind." Rebecca kept tapping her fingers on her napkin.

"Nor should we question her. What business is it of ours?" I demanded.

"I don't agree. We're all grown women and can handle whatever it is. We let it go back then, but I'm not letting it go this time. I think we should all look into it. Who wants to be a part of a family with a bunch of secrets? No ma'am! For all you know, this secret could impact us in some way."

"That's ludicrous. Don't you think it would've impacted us by now? I think you're barking up the wrong tree," I said.

"Payton, I tried my best to console Mom and to ask her about it as gently as I knew how, but all she did was brush me off. Heck, for all we know there could be a love child out there somewhere. We could have another sibling. Besides, Jolene made it my business the moment she blurted out everything in front of me. Especially the part about the neighbor across the street."

"What's the neighbor have to do with anything? A better question might be what does any of this have to do with you?" I slammed my glass down on the table and accidentally splashed wine everywhere.

Abby looked at me with widened eyes. Rebecca lowered her voice and leaned closer in.

"We are family and we all have a right to know. If Mom and Jolene want to flaunt family secrets in front of me, then to heck with it. I'm a lawyer, I can easily find out on my own. How quickly you forget that I own Uncle Samuel's property in Savannah, now. That makes things even easier."

"AND?" Abby questioned sternly.

"And? What do you mean and? Ethan and I fly up a few times a year to check on the property and the renters. You can't blindly trust property management companies these days. That neighbor they're referring to, is my neighbor, now. He's been living in the same house for over thirty years. His name is Jonathan Murphy. His house sits on a few acres so they can't be talking about anyone else but him. And, get this... When I bought Uncle Samuel's fixer upper last year, I met him. He helped to look after the place when it was vacant. He called himself a friend of Uncle Samuel's."

13

"Hooray, for you. So, you happen to know the guy." I leaned back and folded my arms in disgust.

"Payton. I don't think I like your attitude. I'm not the one who's hiding skeletons in the closet," Rebecca said.

"Unbelievable. You realize you're talking about our mother here, right? Don't you think she should be the one to decide how much you know and when you know it?"

"I'm with Payton on this one. You're out of line, Rebecca. You have no business meddling around behind Mom's back and you know it." Abby rolled her eyes.

"You two can gang up on me all you want to. I'm used to it by now. You won't hurt my feelings," she said.

"It's not your feelings I'm worried about. It's Mom's. Think about it. How would you feel if your child went behind your back and dug up your past?" I tried to help her see things differently, but Rebecca was as stubborn as they come. At times, she was so easy to love. Other times, I wondered if we were born from the same woman.

"Payton, this wouldn't happen to me and you know it. I'm an open book. Ask me anything you want to know and I'll tell it, including what Ethan and I did behind closed doors last night."

If I were the physical type, I would've reached across the table and snatched her up by her blouse. In my imagination, a few slaps could easily put the whole thing to rest.

"Abby, maybe you can talk some sense into her. I'm at a loss for words."

Abby let out a deep sigh.

"So much for a relaxing dinner. I would've been better off eating mac and cheese with the kids. Look, Rebecca, you want to know, I get it. I'm curious myself, but not to the extent that I would sabotage Mom over it." Abby tried to reason with her.

"Sabotage? Who said anything about sabotage? I just plan to do a little investigating, that's all. Mom doesn't have to know. She can tell us at some point or not. That's up to her. As a matter of fact, you two don't even have to know. Whether it be a steamy love affair or a long-lost love child involved, I'll just keep it to myself."

I made one last ditch effort to talk her out of it.

"Rebecca, I have to say... I don't know what's gotten into you. I thought you'd become a changed woman after having John William, but maybe I was wrong. For the love of all things good, I'm begging you to please stay out of this. Mom is looking forward to everyone gathering at her house for Christmas in just a few short weeks. The last thing she needs is someone like you ruining everything. Cousin Jolene is already doing a fine job of that all by herself. I'm asking you as kindly as I know how to drop it."

"I said I would leave you out of it, Payton. You won't be the wiser."

The server apologized for taking so long and brought us a few appetizers on the house along with the menus. I didn't have much of an appetite anymore. I found myself staring at the words on the menu, clueless as to what I was reading. My sisters placed their orders first.

"Ma'am, can I interest you in our special for the evening?"

"I'm sorry, what was the special again?"

"The salt-crusted tilapia with lemongrass. You can get it with a side order of..."

"No, thank you. I'm not big on tilapia. If I could just have a steak, well done, with mashed potatoes and green beans that would be fine."

"Alright, one well done steak coming right up. And ladies, I have your orders. I'll be back in a jiffy."

I pushed my appetizer to the side and tried to address Rebecca again. I knew I wasn't wrong about the situation. But Abby jumped in before I could say anything.

"We're not asking you to leave us out of it, Rebecca. We're asking you to leave it alone. I'm also asking both of you to kindly change the subject. I didn't get all dolled up to come out here and have a terrible time. Ya'll know I don't get out much, so I really wish you would just quit already. Agreed?"

Nobody said a word at first. I didn't trust Rebecca as far as I could see her on this matter. But Abby was right. There was no sense in harping on it for the rest of the night. We vocalized our feelings about it. Anything she did going forward was on her.

I buckled myself in and hit the auto-dialer to call Abby on the car ride home. "Dialing Abby," the automated voice announced. I could barely make it out of the parking lot without satisfying my urge to vent.

"Hello?" she answered.

"Has Rebecca lost her mind?"

"I don't know, Payton. I'd like to think she means well. Even if she is going about it the wrong way. The poor girl has the horns that grow out of her head on occasion and they make her act a little crazy."

I never heard Abby refer to Rebecca in that way, but she certainly had her number. Out of the three of us she was definitely the more feisty one. But never once did I think she'd take all that energy and turn it against her own mother.

"Payton, if you want to know the truth, I think this whole thing will die down if we leave it alone. Rebecca can be hot tempered and stubborn, but I don't think she'll bother with it."

"I don't know, Abby."

"Seriously. It was only because we were asking her not to poke around in Mom's business that she was being so fiery about it. I promise if we would've acted nonchalant like we didn't care, she would've lost interest," Abby said.

"That's so stupid. We shouldn't have to play mind games with a thirty-six-year-old to get her to behave."

"We shouldn't but it is what it is. Besides, aren't you just a little curious yourself? I'm not saying Rebecca is going about this the right way, but don't you want to know?"

"Abby, it's crossed my mind, but I'm at peace with not knowing. The way I look at it is if dad was forgiving and let it go, then why can't we? We need to come together as a family now more than ever. Not the opposite."

"True."

"Listen, for now let's just put all of this out of our minds and focus on happier things. Tonight, I want you to go home and spend time with your sweet husband and daughter. This weekend, we'll all drive out to the farm and help Mom pick the most gorgeous tree she's ever had. It will be wonderful. What do you say?" Abby tried to help me look at the bright side.

"Alright, I guess you're right. Christmas has always been my favorite time of the year. Say hello to Wyatt and the kids for me."

"I will. Goodnight, Payton."

"Goodnight."

~

I entered our bedroom door and stepped on a trail of red rose petals. I couldn't imagine what the occasion was. But, I guess with only six months of marriage under our belt, we didn't really need a special occasion. The trail led to the master bath. It was just like Cole to do something sweet and romantic. However, I still considered Emmie's whereabouts before going any further. I turned around to find Cole standing right behind me.

"Cole Miller! You scared the daylights out of me."

"I'm sorry, I didn't mean to. I just wanted to catch your reaction to the surprise. Before you ask about Emmie, I gave her permission to have a sleepover at her friend Madison's house tonight."

"On a school night?"

"Tomorrow is Friday, plus the girls promised to be super responsible and do their homework first. Besides, it's almost time for Christmas break. With all the excitement in the air, I thought it would be nice to let her do something spontaneous."

"But what about her..."

"Relax. Take a deep breath. Everything's covered, I promise. I figured after a night out you'd enjoy coming home to a hot bubbly bath."

How could I resist those cute dimples? Cole had a way of convincing me to do just about anything when he smiled at me.

"Look at you. Your shoulders are tense and you look stressed, Payton. You always work hard to meet our needs, but somebody has to take care of you. Now, I want you to go in there and enjoy the relaxing bath I prepared for you. And, I won't take no for an answer."

"Taking a hot bubble bath does sound rather enticing. There's only one thing I'm curious to know."

He softly kissed my neck.

"What?"

"Do you plan to join me? I mean, since you went to all the trouble of creating a romantic evening, don't you think it would be more fitting for two?"

Cole chuckled.

"I had every intention of making this evening all about you. Of course, if you're extending an invitation, I won't say no to my beautiful wife."

Maybe it was silly, but I still felt butterflies every time Cole flirted with me. I finally put to rest everything that irritated me about this evening and focused on spending a little quality time with my husband.

ABBY

*E*very year it was a tradition to pack everyone in the Suburban and drive sixty miles to the countryside in search for the perfect tree. As a young girl, I recalled having the task of searching for two trees. One to stand tall at the entrance of the inn, and the second tree about six feet tall, to rest perfectly by the fireplace at the cottage. The inn was no longer a part of our lives, but my sisters and I thought it might be fun to keep up with the tradition for Mom and Dad.

We turned down the long gravel driveway leading up to the farm. The aroma of pine and spruce filled the air. I could barely put the truck in park before the kids were unbuckling their seat belts.

"Alright, Aiden and Maggie, I don't have a problem with you looking around but make sure you stick together."

"Okay."

The kids ran off, leaving myself, Mom, Payton, and Rebecca to stretch and get our bearings.

"Mom, what did you have in mind for this year? Do you think you might want another pine, or a spruce, or..." Payton started strolling beside Mom toward the trees.

"Oh, I don't know. The tree has to speak to me. There has to be a connection. I'll know it when I see it," she said.

"Interesting. I usually go with one that's well rounded and doesn't look like it's dying. But, hey, I guess we all have our thing," Rebecca said as she trailed behind to check her cell phone.

"Rebecca, it wouldn't hurt to unplug for a little while and be in the moment," I said.

"I am in the moment, Abby. I just needed to make sure I completed the online check in for our flight tomorrow afternoon."

"Tomorrow afternoon? Where are you going just two weeks before Christmas?"

"Ethan and I are taking a quick trip to Savannah. We originally planned to go check on things after the new year, but it turns out the trip had to be moved up."

"Why, what's the urgency?"

"Well, for one, our renters took off and left the place vacant. This doesn't surprise me because they were getting way behind in their rent. But we received a phone call from the management company because several things were missing from the house."

"What could possibly be missing besides their belongings?"

"The appliances, a couple of chandeliers, you know... the typical stuff that normally gets left behind when you move out of a house."

"No way! I'm sorry. Where did you find these people?" We

paused behind Mom and Payton as they were observing the first tree.

"Through the management company. Perhaps it wasn't the best move in hindsight. But, it's too late now. We're just going to fly up and meet the contractors and then we'll go from there."

"Man, you guys just completed the renovations not too long ago. Sorry to hear that."

"Sorry to hear what?" Payton asked.

"Just a little trouble with our first round of renters. We're going to fly to Savannah and get things straightened out tomorrow. It's no big deal." Rebecca brushed it off and started looking at the trees with Mom.

Payton and I looked at each other.

"Good morning, ladies. Can I help you?" A tall man with the build of a lumberjack greeted us over by the pines.

"Perfect timing. My name is Helen Matthews. How are you?"

"I'm doing pretty well, ma'am. My name is Dave Carrolton of Carrolton Farms. How can I help you today?"

Mom's face lit up like it was Christmas morning. I think coming out here definitely brought back fond memories for her just as much as it did for the rest of us.

"In all the years we've been coming here, I don't think I've ever met you, Mr. Carrolton. What a treat. I can't wait to tell my husband."

"Please, call me Dave. The pleasure is all mine. We have a lot of staff members who help out at the farm. But, it's always a pleasure when I have a chance to meet our customers first hand."

While they were talking, I overheard Payton asking Rebecca more questions.

"So, did you reconsider what we talked about the other day?" Payton placed her hands in her front pockets and had a confident stance as she waited for Rebecca to respond.

"I'm not sure what you're talking about. What exactly do you want me to reconsider?" Rebecca responded in a sarcastic tone.

"Really?"

"Yes, really. There's nothing for me to reconsider."

"Oh, so does that mean you're going to drop the whole thing?"

"I didn't say that either. I'm just not discussing it with you anymore. You weren't exactly supportive, so I figured the best thing to do was not talk about it at all."

"Girls, come over here. Look at this one. I think I found the tree." Mom waved us down, but I was reluctant to leave Payton and Rebecca. They sounded like they were just moments away from needing a referee.

"Hey, I thought we all agreed to leave it alone for now. We're here for Mom, remember? Put on a cheerful smile and get yourselves over there and help her with the tree," I said in an assertive tone.

Payton walked off, but Rebecca lingered and rolled her eyes. I took this as my cue to go looking for the kids.

"Maggie... Aiden... where are you?"

"Right here, Momma." They dodged from in between the trees.

"We saw the most gigantic tree ever. It was almost as tall as our house," Aiden said with all the enthusiasm a six-year-old could muster up.

"Wow, that's pretty big. You'll have to show it to me. I think Gram found a tree that she likes, too."

"Actually, I found two trees. It's down to the Leyland Cypress or the Southern Red Cedar. I love both of them and can't seem to decide."

"I vote for the Leyland. It's nice and full," Payton said as she inspected the back of the tree.

"Clearly you overlooked the Southern Red Cedar. The quality is ten times better and I'll bet it will last longer," Rebecca said with opposition.

"You two are no help. How about we ask the grandkids what they think. Maggie... Aiden... Gram needs help choosing a tree. Would you go with the one Aunt Payton is standing next to? Or would you choose the one next to Aunt Rebecca?"

"I like the one next to Aunt Payton." Maggie ran over and stood next to Payton.

"Yeah, me, too," Aiden agreed.

Payton could've easily gloated in front of Rebecca, but she didn't. She was mature beyond her years and sought to bring the best out of people and not the worst.

"Ladies, can I interest you in some hot cocoa while you wait for us to prepare the tree?"

"That sounds like a wonderful idea," I said.

"Great. If you head over to the farmhouse, my wife will be waiting for you. She just made a fresh batch. We have a little gift shop inside if you want to take a look around. As soon as we have the tree mounted on the top of your truck I'll come and get you." Dave pointed toward a white house with a porch swing just across the yard.

They set the old farmhouse up like a retail store inside. Every ounce of the place was decorated for Christmas. It felt like a workshop for Santa and his little helpers. The kids were busy digging for ornaments in wicker baskets, and the rest of us were sipping our cocoa while admiring all the holiday trinkets.

"Abby, don't you just love what they've done with the place? It's so dreamy. If we stayed here all day, I still don't think we'd get to see everything. I should bring Cole and Emmie next year," Payton said.

"Come to think of it, why didn't you bring them this year? We could've followed each other in two separate cars."

"They had special plans to go Christmas shopping this morning. I was told that it was for daddys and daughters only. I wasn't allowed to go."

"You know what that means."

"Yep. They're shopping for me." Payton smiled.

Rebecca wandered around the store but continued to be more engaged on her phone than anything else. I overheard her making several calls about her rental house in Georgia.

After having brunch in town, we headed back to Pelican Beach. The plan for the afternoon was to help Mom set the tree up and elicit help from Cousin Jolene to put on the finishing touches while we hung all the outdoor wreaths. Rebecca announced that she would leave early to prepare for her trip.

"Do you think you could at least help us get the tree in the house before you leave?" I asked.

"Yeah, as long as we get right to it. I have to get home and pack plus do a million other things if we're going to make this flight in the morning," she said.

"Rebecca, is everything alright? You've been rather distracted all day." Mom sounded concerned.

"I'm fine. I just have a lot on my plate with the rental and a few other obligations. It's not a big deal."

"Okay, if you say so. You just don't seem like yourself, so whatever it is, I hope it gets resolved soon. While I have all of you here I want to confirm that we're still planning for Christmas dinner at my house this year, right?"

"Yes, Mother." We all chimed.

"Only if you promise to let us help you." I knew that Mom would try to outdo herself as she had always done in the past. But there was no reason for it with three capable daughters. Each of us could bring a dish or two and help lighten the load.

"Don't you worry. There's plenty for you to do. And, don't forget we have Jolene to help this year." Mom put on her glasses and started making notes on her memo pad.

"How are things going with you two?" I asked.

"She's been a big help with your father. We bump heads occasionally, but that's nothing new."

"That's not what I saw the other day," Rebecca mumbled under her breath.

Mom lowered her head and looked over the trim of her glasses to address Rebecca.

"Do you care to explain yourself?"

"I said that's not what I saw the other day. It looked as if she was drinking, embarrassing you, and airing out all of your dirty laundry. Surely, you remember. I tried to come to your aid, but you snapped at me and told me to hush and stay out of it, remember?"

"Ahem." Payton cleared her throat.

Mom slowly turned around and looked out the passenger's

window. I continued to focus on the road but there was no mistaking that Rebecca's comment created a little tension.

"As I said before, we bump heads at times but she's been a big help," Mom concluded.

The lyrics to my favorite Christmas song faded to silence. It was obvious that Mom wasn't going to engage with Rebecca. Anyone with common sense would take that as a cue to leave the subject matter alone. At least that's what we did as kids growing up. Whenever we touched on a sore subject the adults didn't want to talk about, we left it alone. Well, at least Payton and I did. Rebecca was always on a mission to self-destruct.

"Who's ready to help put up the tree at Gram's house?"

I figured it was time for a change in subject. I'd do anything to help shift the mood back to all things merry.

"Me!" The kids, Payton, and Mom were all for it.

"As much as I'd love to hang out with my favorite niece and nephew, I should really get home." Rebecca continued emailing and texting just as she had done all day.

"Aunt Becca, don't you want to help put the star at the top of the tree? If you don't come, you're going to miss out on the best part of decorating," Aiden said.

"Aww, I'll get to see the star when I get back, buddy. Maybe you can take a picture and get Mom to send it to my phone."

"Okay."

"Rebecca, what's Ethan's parents doing for Christmas? You know they're more than welcome to join us," Mom said as I pulled up to Rebecca's driveway.

"I'll check with him and let you know," she said while opening the car door.

"Okay, have a safe flight tomorrow. Let us know when you

land safely." Mom barely finished her words before Rebecca closed the door and began marching toward the house.

"I wonder what's gotten into her lately. I don't even know why she bothered to come if all she was going to do was be on her phone and have an attitude most of the day."

"Mom, do you think it might have anything to do with the way you spoke to her when she was trying to help you the other day? I'm not taking sides or anything, but she really seemed offended," Payton said.

"Offended? Oh, please. I was preventing her from making things worse. Jolene doesn't need anyone to egg her on once she's had a few. She can be a wrecking ball without having help from Rebecca. Plus, I wasn't going to stand by and let her give me the third degree about a stupid remark made by Jolene."

"Okay, I can't help it, Mom. I'm still trying my best to understand your reasoning behind having Jolene at the cottage. Is she really as helpful as you say she is? Or are you just afraid that if she leaves we're going to throw you and Daddy in a nursing home?" I was convinced it was the latter. I just had to put it out there to see what Mom would say. If I were in her shoes, there's no way I could put up with that woman on a regular basis. Jolene would drive me to check into a mental institution.

"Come on, tell the truth, Mom. Is that your fear?"

"No, Abby. For heaven's sake, I'm not worried about anybody throwing me into a nursing home."

"Okay, fine. Well, at least tell me you're happy, and she's not taking over and running amuck."

"She's not. We had a nice little talk recently to help set things in order."

"Okay. You mean, set things in order, as in, she's going to stop drinking?" Payton asked.

"Well, I didn't say all that. But we definitely have an established agreement that's working for all parties involved. Now, if we could ever so kindly change the subject, I would greatly appreciate it. The only thing that's on my mind is putting up the finishing touches of my decorations. Once the tree is trimmed and the wreaths are hung, I'll finally start to feel like things are in order for Christmas."

"Okay. You won't hear another word from me unless it has to do with Christmas and decorations," Payton said.

"Christmas, decorations, and more hot chocolate and cookies!" Maggie said.

"That's right. More hot chocolate and cookies. How could I forget?"

PAYTON

ith only nine days left until Christmas, my assistant Natalie and I were working hard to prepare the store for the new year. It was hard not to daydream and get lost in the holiday spirit, but so much needed to be done. I stared over at the electronic Mr. and Mrs. Claus in my window display while trying to orchestrate my to do list.

"Payton, can I interest you in some coffee? I don't know about you, but I'm feeling awfully sleepy this morning. Maybe it's the overcast skies that's making me so tired."

"You know what, Natalie, that doesn't sound like a bad idea. I might need a large cup so I can wake up and stop staring at Mr. Claus shaking his rear end."

"Ha, no problem. One large cup coming right up."

The coo-coo clock chimed to announce it was 9:25 a.m. I never did figure out how to get that clock to act right, but it still added charm.

For the past six months, Natalie had been working as my

full-time assistant. I don't know where I'd be without her. She was detail oriented and reliable... the kind of employee every business owner dreamed of having. My only wish was for her to live a normal life. Natalie's mother was terribly sick, so she spent most of her time caring for her when she wasn't working with me. If only she could get out every once in a while. I think it would do her some good.

I glanced over to see her climbing a tall ladder with a feather duster in hand.

"Hey, Payton. When I'm done with these shelves, what did you have in mind for me to work on today?"

"Well, since it's so slow I thought we could look at marking down some of our inventory. I can make a note of the new prices in the system while you make the adjustments on our website."

"I'll get right on it."

"Oh, and maybe we can run a few specials for the new year. Once January 1st hits, everyone will be more concerned with gym memberships and resolutions more than anything else."

"Ha! Don't worry. It won't last long. Just as quickly as everyone makes a resolution they usually forget about it. I'm sure you'll have plenty of photoshoots in the new year to keep you busy."

"True. Natalie, I know your birthday is coming up soon. Are you making any plans to celebrate?"

"Not really. I'll probably stick close to home to look after Mom. Maybe I'll pick up some takeout on the way in, but that's about it."

"I don't know her very well, but I'm sure your mother would want you to have a little fun. We should plan something together, like ice skating. Maybe we could even take a drive and see the Christmas lights on Main Street on the way to the skating rink. Please say yes, it's my treat!"

"It sounds nice, but I can't. Even if I went, I wouldn't be any fun. I'd probably just feel guilty."

"Oh, but the views of the Christmas lights are spectacular. At least take the drive with me. Your mom could even come along if she's feeling up to it."

"We'll see. Some days are better than others."

Most days Natalie put on a good show at work, but I had a feeling things were worse than she was letting on.

"What about celebrating with a simple cake here at the store? It's better than doing nothing."

She cracked a brief smile.

"That might be nice."

"I don't want to pry, Natalie. Just know that I'm here if you ever need someone to talk to. I'd hate to see your birthday and the holidays come and go without you having some level of enjoyment. This year my family is celebrating Christmas at my parents' house. We're planning to make it a big celebration. Mom's philosophy has always been, the more the merrier. Even if it's just for a little while, we'd love to have you stop by."

She climbed down the stepladder, while still holding the duster in hand.

"That's kind of you, Payton. I haven't really been in the Christmas spirit this year. When I'm here at the store it helps to take my mind off things for a little while. But mostly, we haven't been playing music, decorating, or doing anything that reminds me of the holidays. We don't even have a tree this year. And I definitely don't have any nice clothes to wear to your family gathering or gifts to bring. I thank you for thinking of me, though. It's awfully nice of you."

Natalie's words broke my heart. The last thing we cared about was appearances or gifts.

"Awe, Natalie, my invitation doesn't come with strings attached. We're not looking for gifts and nobody is getting dressed up. Well, I take that back. Cousin Jolene might wear a bunch of floral prints from top to bottom, and Mom will be the only one with pearls on, but the rest of us like to hang out in jeans."

Natalie laughed.

"Does she really wear that much floral print?"

"She wears that much of any print. Then there's the beehive hairdo and let's not forget her accent. If you think it's funny now, wait until you meet her in person. Don't say I didn't tell you so."

"She sounds funny."

"She's more than funny. I probably should be embarrassed to have you around her, but I'm praying she'll behave herself in front of company."

"I'm sure it will be fun. But, again, I'll have to wait and see how Mom feels. If she's up for it, then we'll be there."

"That's wonderful. I'll let the family know to prepare for extra guests just in case."

She brought the laptop closer so we could work on the markdowns.

"Natalie."

"Yes."

"There's one last thing on my mind."

"Sure, what's up?"

"Earlier you mentioned something about not having a Christmas tree."

"Oh, it's no big deal. This year things are a little tight, but we'll be fine. As long as Mom and I have each other. That's what's most important, right?"

"Yes. Always. But... I couldn't imagine a Christmas without a tree to celebrate with. I could be wrong, but I bet you feel the same way. I guess it's all about the memories you create more than anything else. If you would allow me to, I'd love to help you find the perfect tree."

"I couldn't, Payton. It's a sweet gesture, but you've already done so much for me. The last thing I want to do is become a charity case."

"I don't think of you as a charity case at all. Honestly, I think you are a strong young lady who's holding it all together. But that doesn't mean that every now and again someone can't do something nice for you."

She shook her head as if she were going to resist.

"Just hear me out, and if you don't like my idea, I promise I won't mention another word about it."

"Okay."

"Look at that coo-coo clock hanging on the wall."

"Yeah."

"And this rotary phone, and the Christmas tree. Oh, let's not forget Mr. and Mrs. Claus," I said while pointing to the decorations around the room.

"What about it?"

"Do you remember me telling you where it all came from?"

A smile slowly rose on her face.

"The thrift shop?"

"That's right! My absolute favorite place to find little odds and ends."

"Payton, you're a genius. How come I didn't think of this!"

"I don't know. Sometimes you just need to open up and talk, girl. That way you can bounce a few ideas around. I think I told you a long time ago about my little hobby. I love collecting vintage items from the thrift shop. I get excited at the thought of wandering around and looking for treasures. The last time I was there, I saw plenty of Christmas trees. Some were six to eight feel tall. Why don't we head over there after work to see what we can find?"

"I guess I could go look. Mom would definitely be surprised if I came home with a tree."

"I bet she would. It would be my pleasure to treat you to it. I'm sure they have garland and even a wreath or two if you're interested."

"Payton, after all you've done for me, I just don't understand it."

"And you don't have to. Just say yes... please."

"Yes, I'll go. We'll see about the tree when we get there."

"Okay."

Later that evening we left the thrift store with a tree, several ornaments, and new lights for Natalie. I even found a vintage Christmas village to set up at the store. As if I needed any more decorations. I helped Natalie carry the tree up to the front porch of an old two-story house. I wasn't sure who they were renting the place from, but it looked as if the landlord hadn't painted or replaced the siding in years. A part of me wanted to stick around to meet her mother and see her reaction. But, since Natalie appeared to be in a hurry to get inside, I thought better of it and wished her a good evening.

The melody of Dad's diesel engine hummed all the way to my parents' driveway. I'd recently started driving his car to keep it in good running condition. We were hoping to sell it soon to someone who was into maintaining classic cars.

Outside the front door, I could hear music blaring to the tune of Santa Baby. It didn't take much guessing to figure out who the culprit was.

I lifted the needle to my parents' old record player. They were probably one of the last few generations in the family that preserved and played records. Jolene was sitting upright in my father's chair with her head hung over, fast asleep with a glass in hand.

"Cousin Jolene, wake up," I whispered.

"Huh? What you say? Shoot first, ask questions later!"

"Cousin Jolene, you must be dreaming. It's me, Payton."

"Payton?"

"Yes, Payton. Where is everybody? And why are you sitting out here playing the music so loud?"

"Well, howdy to you, too. I was just entertaining myself and having a little nightcap before I head upstairs. Helen and William went up already. I tell you, those two go to bed with the chickens. I'm more of a night owl. Hey, what time is it, anyway?"

"It's seven o'clock. Way too early for anyone to be in bed if you ask me, but what do I know."

I inhaled the aroma of the Leland Cypress while admiring its beauty.

"Can I offer you a drink?"

"No, thank you. I really don't drink much outside the occasional glass of wine."

"Well then pour some wine. Relax instead of pacing around here with your hands in your pockets. I'll tell you, Payton, you're just like your mother. Both of you are kindhearted but way too straight laced for me. Go on and pour a glass and have a seat. It won't hurt for you to stay and talk to your Cousin Jolene for a little while."

"I really can't stay that long. I just stopped by to drop off a few items for Mom. Cole and Emmie are waiting for me."

"Right. I didn't think you'd stay, anyway."

"What is that supposed to mean?"

"Oh, nothing worth talking about," she said as she took her time getting up out of the chair.

"You might as well say it."

"You and your sisters... it's pretty clear you're not fond of me being here, but I thought we'd be past that by now."

"Cousin Jolene, I..."

"No, no, no. You don't have to explain. I get it. Nobody wants an old crazy lady around."

I didn't know how to respond, but it was obvious she wanted company, so I sat down. I guess I hadn't invested in spending much personal time with her, but it was mainly because she was always doing or saying something outlandish.

"Mom talks about how helpful it's been to have you around all the time."

She poured more of the brown-colored beverage in her glass and took a sip. You could tell she was savoring the taste before she spoke.

"I'm glad to help. Your father still does a lot for himself. He may need a reminder or two... heck, maybe even three. But he's not doing too bad. All he ever wants to do is sit in front of the television all day. I have to pry him out of the house to get some fresh air."

"And what about you?"

"I spend my days looking after Will. I can't say that I have much more to tell."

"I don't believe that for one minute, Cousin Jolene. You're sitting out here in the living room drinking by yourself. Surely something must be on your mind."

"Hmm, I guess old habits die hard. My husband and I used to conclude the evening in the living room together before heading to bed. He would play the nightly news and nod off to sleep in his recliner, and I'd do the same until about eleven o'clock. Then he'd tap me on the shoulder and say, 'Shug, it's time to head to bed.' Shug was the nickname he had for me, short for Sugar."

She threw her head back to swallow the rest of her drink before putting her glass down and continuing to speak.

"Sometimes we'd go to bed and head straight to sleep. Other times, we'd lie there and talk until it was almost sunrise. Those were the good old days. I miss my best friend. Guess you wouldn't remember too much about George. You girls spent the most time around him when you were little, way before your parents purchased the inn."

"I vaguely remember him. But I'm sure he meant the world to you."

We sat quietly for a few minutes. I wondered if the source of Jolene's drinking had to do with missing her husband. I also wondered if she'd get around to talking about Mom's past the same way she did around Rebecca. I wouldn't press the issue like my sister, but if Cousin Jolene mentioned anything, I might listen. Perhaps that made me just as bad as Rebecca.

"We used to have a blast back then. We'd all play cards together, have cookouts, and even take road trips together. We were the four musketeers. Will and George used to argue over who was driving. It never failed. It was so funny. We could always count on an argument out of the two of them like clockwork and before you could blink good, they'd be over it and on to something else." It tickled her pink just talking about it.

"I heard you used to take trips to Georgia. Did you know that Rebecca bought Uncle Samuel's house? I think it's the same place you used to visit if I have the story right."

Her facial expression turned more serious.

"Yep, it's the same place. Good old Uncle Sammy. It was always a good time whenever we went to visit. He had so much room in that big old house we could get lost in it. Did I hear you mention that Rebecca bought it?"

"She did. She and Ethan turned it into a rental property. Even though I'm not so sure it's going very well. Uncle Samuel left the house to his daughters, but they didn't do anything with it. They tried to pass it on to the three of us, but Abby and I didn't want the responsibility. Rebecca didn't let that stop her. She took on the house by herself and renovated it and even befriended the neighbor across the street to help her out. She's a real go-getter when she puts her mind to something."

"The neighbor across the street? You mean John?"

"I don't remember his name. You'd have to ask Rebecca. Why? Do you know him?"

"I haven't spoken to him in years, but let's just say everyone in the community knew each other very well. I mean... very well. We used to drive up to catch the annual summer festival and then turn around and go back for fall harvest. I'm sure your mother could tell you plenty of stories."

Mom walked in with her rollers and her night robe on.

"Ahem, Jolene. Isn't it getting late? I thought surely you'd be enjoying your nightcap upstairs like we agreed?"

I hopped up from the couch. It felt like we were doing something wrong with the way she walked in. Jolene didn't move an inch. Instead, she checked her glass and laid it back down again.

"Ah, yes, that's right. The house rules. How could I forget?" Jolene's speech sounded sloppy.

The entire exchange was rather interesting. It felt like Mom was cracking a whip for Jolene to remember her place. Like there was something more that she wanted to say but couldn't. If that was the case, maybe their living arrangement wasn't as cozy as Mom wanted us to believe.

"Payton, I didn't know you were here. Why didn't you come upstairs to get me?" She reached out to give me a hug.

"Cousin Jolene told me you were heading to bed. I didn't want to disturb you. I just stopped by to drop off a few things from the store. Everything is in the bag over there. Cousin Jolene was kind enough to invite me to sit down for a minute, but I really need to get home."

"Well, that's too bad. I'd much rather join in on the conversation down here than listen to your father snore. What were you two talking about?"

"Ha! Wouldn't you like to know," Jolene said.

"Nothing important, Mom. I really need to get home to Cole and Emmie. I promise I'll be back within the next day or so to check on you. The next time we talk, I was hoping we could get a shopping list together for Christmas dinner."

"Yes, we need to work on the list," she said.

"Don't worry, I'm on it. Oh, and before I forget, it's not guaranteed, but we may have two potential guests. I invited Natalie to come with her mother, if she's feeling up to it."

"Wonderful! The more the merrier!"

"I told her you would say that."

I waved goodbye to Jolene on the way out the door. She looked like she was minutes from falling right back into the deep coma that I found her in when I arrived.

ALICE

"*S*tanley, your hot chocolate is ready. I added marshmallows just the way you like it."

"Thank you, darling, may I have some sugar first?"

"Sugar in your hot chocolate?"

"No, I want some sugar from my wife. Then I can enjoy the hot chocolate after."

"Stanley, you're such a flirt."

"Aren't newlyweds supposed to flirt? It's not my fault you're running around here looking so scrumptious."

"Now, now, tiger.... how about a little sugar for now, and some later after we finish wrapping the gifts?"

It was the weekend before Thanksgiving that I had the privilege of becoming Mrs. Holcomb. Stanley and I planned to have an intimate wedding with just the immediate family before the end of the year. Cole and Payton wouldn't hear of it. The kids invited guests, family came from out of town, and before we knew what hit us, we were having a full-blown wedding. Not to mention that all of this took place while Stanley had his house on the market. It was pure insanity. All the packing and moving nearly sucked the life out of us. But we did it, and I have to admit, it was all worth it.

It's been interesting getting to know the other side of Stanley's personality. I'm discovering all the things you don't really see until you're living together. I think it's sweet, really. Not a day goes by where he doesn't take his shoes off in the same spot, hum while brushing his teeth, and find something to fix at his workbench every single day.

"Alice, I could've sworn we wrapped at least ten boxes yesterday. How many more do we have to go? The bigger question is how in the world did you have time to buy all this stuff?"

"Thankfully, I could order a lot of it online. What can I say? The family is growing by the minute. If we're going over to Helen's house on Christmas day, I can't show up empty-handed. Then there are the gifts that still need to be mailed to your side of the family."

"Don't worry about spoiling my side of the family. Growing up, we had a rule that we lived by for gift giving. The adults stopped buying gifts for each other and focused whatever extra funds they had on the kids. That way it helped to cut down on the expenses. The way they hike these prices up for the holidays is just ridiculous. These retailers ought to be ashamed of themselves."

"I wish you would've told me a lot sooner. Oh, well. We'll figure it out."

"Let's see what we have here. Mens ties, an assortment of gourmet tea bags, and golf balls. Who are these gifts for?" he asked while pulling down another sheet of wrapping paper.

"The ties are for your nephews, the tea assortment is a

stocking stuffer for Aunt Mae, and the golf balls are for your brother Joe. They're just little gifts to let them know you're thinking about them, that's all."

Stanley chuckled.

"I'm sure they'll get a kick out of this when they open up the mailbox. They'll definitely know this was not my doing."

"I signed both of our names on the card."

He laughed even harder.

"The mere fact that they're receiving anything will let them know it was your doing, but I don't mind. The way you put your loving touch on everything makes it even more special. Thank you, Alice."

"Are you sure you're okay with it? I'd hate to change the way you're accustomed to doing things."

"I don't mind at all."

"Alright."

I passed him the scissors.

"Alice, I rode over to the house yesterday to pick up the last few pieces of mail. It looks like the buyers are all settled in."

"I've been meaning to ask you about that. How does it feel to ride by your old place knowing it's not yours anymore?"

"It didn't bother me at all. I have the military to thank for that. After spending years moving from place to place, one more move wasn't going to hurt me."

I put my bows down to cuddle with Stanley.

"That's what I love most about you. Your heart is so open and ready for the next adventure that awaits you."

"As long as the adventure involves having you by my side."

"Do you know what I'm considering right now?"

"The way you keep inching closer to me, I might have an idea."

"How about we save the rest of these gifts for later this evening? I think we need some more of that sugar you were talking about earlier."

"You don't have to tell me twice."

~

Later we drove to Pelican Beach to visit with Cole, Payton, and my granddaughter, Emmie.

Emmie was wiping the table down when we entered the kitchen. She had her apron on and flour smeared across her cheek. Watching her brought back fond memories of how we used to cook together. It was no surprise to see her taking the lead in the kitchen.

"Payton, it looks like you and Cole have a master chef on your hands. I love her confidence. Just look at her cooking and cleaning! Anytime you want to send her our way, we'd welcome the extra help."

"Alice, we owe it all to you. I can tell Emmie has spent a lot of time under your tutelage. Emmie, why don't you tell your grandma and Stanley what's on the menu for dinner."

"Sure, tonight for your dining pleasure, we're having homemade pizza, with a tossed salad on the side. The pies are in the oven, so it shouldn't take long to bake."

"Emmie, it smells delicious," Stanley said while he was taking off his jacket.

"Thanks, Stanley. A little birdie told me you like pepperoni, so I covered one pie with pepperoni just for you."

"You and I are going to get along very well, young lady."

Cole gave Stanley a bear hug.

"How are the newlyweds doing?" He smiled. I loved the

way he welcomed Stanley into the family. Witnessing the way they've been bonding has truly been heartwarming for me.

"We're well. I guess we could ask you the same thing," Stanley said.

"No complaints on my end. Just trying to keep up with the demands of the business while helping Payton get ready for the holidays."

"One would think Cole's renovation projects would start slowing down around Christmas. He's literally been taking calls nonstop. I'm wondering if his clients plan on celebrating Christmas at all," Payton said while she pulled a few glasses out of the cabinet. I noticed her skin looked pale, like a ghost.

"Hey, Mom, can you help me find the seasoning for the salad dressing?"

"Sure, Emmie. Let's see what we have in this cabinet over here."

The more I watched Payton, the more I wondered if she was feeling alright. She was wearing a stained sweatsuit, her hair was in a messy bun, she walked around barefoot, and she looked rather sickly. She was in her own house and could dress however she pleased. It just wasn't like her.

"Payton, how about you? Has the store been keeping you busy?" I asked.

"We've had plenty of traffic popping in to purchase Christmas gifts. The keepsake ornaments have been selling like hotcakes. Who doesn't love an ornament with a photo in it? Having Natalie helps a great deal. I couldn't imagine trying to run the store by myself."

"I'm glad. She's always been a great help to you."

She cleared her throat a few times and began sipping on a can of ginger ale.

"Payton, I have to admit, I'm so excited about having Christmas dinner at your parents' house this year. We've already started wrapping our gifts. Isn't that right, Stanley?"

"Please. Don't even say the word gift or wrapping. If I didn't know any better, I'd think I married Mrs. Claus."

Cole nodded his head.

"Yep, that's Mom for you. If you're not careful she'll hold you hostage. As a kid, I used to make up excuses just so I didn't have to sit around wrapping presents all day."

"And it never worked. I was always on to you, Cole."

"You sure were. My poor fingers almost fell off, but we got the job done."

"Oh stop, it wasn't that bad."

Payton helped Emmie remove the pizza out of the oven. No sooner than she placed it on the counter, it looked like it was all Payton could do to keep from gagging.

"I'm sorry, y'all. I'm not feeling very well. I thought the ginger ale would help, but I think I need to go lay down for a bit. Please help yourself to the pizza."

She quickly exited the kitchen and Cole followed behind her.

"Well, Emmie, I feel just fine. How about yourself?"

"I'm starving. Stanley, how do you feel?" she asked.

"I feel like having a slice of pizza."

"If Payton said we should eat, then I propose we dig in. Why don't you grab the salad, and I'll grab the pizza cutter."

"Yes, ma'am."

We set up everything on the table, and Cole joined us just in time to say grace.

"Thank you, Lord, for this food, for our family, and for our blessings. Please touch Payton with your healing hands so she can feel better soon. Amen."

"Amen." Everyone repeated.

"Cole, how's she doing up there?" I asked.

"She looks like she's about to turn three shades of green, but she's lying down for now. I told her I would check on her in a little while. I'm just hoping she didn't catch a stomach bug."

"Same here. You never want to be sick, but especially around the holidays," Stanley said.

I didn't want to speculate, so I kept my thoughts to myself. But there was another type of bug that newlyweds caught after spending quality time together. It usually had a way of sneaking up on you when you least expected, and it lasted about nine months. That's how it was for me when I found out I was pregnant with Cole. That was over forty-three years ago. Women today seem to have everything carefully planned out, so maybe it was just an upset stomach. I didn't want to come off like a nosey mother-in-law, but it sure would be nice if my suspicions were correct.

"So how's it going over at the house? If you're wrapping Christmas gifts, I can imagine you've unpacked everything and you're starting to feel settled in?" Cole asked.

"Yes, finally, but if it wasn't for your help, I'd probably still be unloading boxes. I can't thank you enough, Cole."

"No thanks needed. It was the least I could do."

"You know, Cole, it's been nice to see you come around, and make me feel like a welcomed member of the family. It means a lot to me."

"I'm glad you feel that way, Stanley. I can admit that I was being way too overprotective when we first met. The most important thing is I see the way you make my mother happy.

You bring out the best in her. And, I've always told you if she's happy, then that makes me happy, too."

"And now we're all one big happy family," Emmie said.

We smiled at Emmie's sweet innocence. She was right. We were one big happy family. After many years of missing my late husband at the table, and Cole's late wife, Laura, we had finally found a way, not to replace their love, but to love again.

REBECCA

"*R*ebecca, it's nice to finally meet in person, I'm John Murphy."

"Yes, John. I recognize your voice from our telephone conversations. Nice to meet you. This is my husband, Ethan."

John stood in the driveway, extending his hand to Ethan. He was a tall white-haired gentleman who spoke with a cigarette hanging out of his mouth. Sort of grungy looking. He stood with his rake in hand and dressed like he was ready to do yard work.

"It looks like you've been mighty busy over here with all the contractors. When you called last week, I know you said the house needed repairs, but goodness! Is it that bad?"

"Mr. Murphy, bad is an understatement. It appears my renters helped themselves to almost everything but the kitchen sink."

"Please, call me John."

Pizza Hut #008009
COUNTER

Ticket # 0022

Item Count: 3

ENTERED BY
  Artannabella
008009   01/16/24   01:50PM

LESLIE

01	1	Medium	12.99
		Pan	
		Cheese	
		Onions	
		Mushrooms	
02	1	Medium	13.99
		Thin	
		Meat Lvr	
		SquareCut	
03	1	Order	4.99
		BreadStx	

	Subtotal	31.97
	SALES TAX	1.92
	Balance Due	33.89

ICONIC CHECK
YOUR ORDER WAS CHECKED BY:

The Hut is hiring!

Visit jobs.pizzahut.com to apply

APPLY NOW

Hut Rewards®

Get your faves for FREE in as few as 2-3 visits.
Visit Pizzahut.com/rewards to join.

SIGN UP NOW

Download the Pizza Hut app.

It's the easiest way to order, reorder, find deals, and so much more.

"John, did you know anything about the people who were renting from me? Did you ever talk to them much?"

"Every once in a while I would run into the wife or the kids at the mailbox. They mostly stayed to themselves. The husband would leave in the morning and return in the evening. I assumed he had a job. The wife stayed home with the kids. I'm just trying to figure out when they left out of here with all your stuff. I didn't hear anything that would make me suspicious. One evening last week I looked out the window and noticed the house looked dark like nobody was home. It's been that way ever since. It's like they disappeared into thin air."

"Interesting."

"They were interesting alright. Every once in a while they did things that caught my attention. But, never anything worth calling you about."

"Like what?"

"She used to have trucks come and drop off large pallets. The pallets were so big she'd have to empty the contents out by hand and load everything into the garage. One time I asked her about it and she told me she sold products online. She was quick to change the subject, like she didn't want to talk about it. So, I just left it alone. Sometimes the trucks would come and pick up boxes from the house. I figured, hey... everybody has a different way of earning income. Who was I to get into their business? In hindsight, maybe she wasn't just shipping off items for her business."

"Maybe. We've already filed a report with the police, but I'd like to share what you just told us if you don't mind," Ethan said.

"No, not at all. Happy to help in any way I can. I'm

assuming they didn't leave any clues as to where they were heading?"

"Not one," I replied.

John scratched his head as if he didn't know what to make of it. I thought this was normally the kind of thing homeowners did when the house was up for foreclosure. I've even heard of renters messing up the place but stealing fixtures out of the house... I don't know what to make of it. And for a family to do such a thing really didn't seem to make any sense to me. Guess I had my work cut out for me if I was going to learn to be a better landlord.

"Rebecca, I'm going to leave you two here to catch up and head back in to check on the guys. John, again, it was nice meeting you."

"Likewise, Ethan."

"Ethan, when you get a chance, please call your mom and check on John William. Tell her I'll call her later on this evening."

"Will do."

I walked with John to the end of the driveway and surveyed our surroundings. In the middle of his yard across the street was a beautiful weeping willow tree with a tire swing hanging from it. It looked like the perfect place for children to play and use their imagination.

"I bet your family has created a ton of sweet memories underneath that willow tree. It looks so picturesque."

"Family, friends, you name it. We've had good times over the years. Those three acres have served us well."

"My goodness. Three acres? Do you live there with your wife?"

"My wife passed away several years ago."

"I'm sorry, Mr. Murphy. I mean... John. I didn't mean to pry."

"You're not prying. Your Uncle Samuel and I were really close. That makes you practically like family. As for the property, I always promised myself that I'd stay until I got to the place where I couldn't take care of it anymore. With a little help from my landscapers, I'd say it's still in pretty good shape."

"I'd say so as well. It's beautiful. Mind if I join you to look around?"

"No, be my guest. It's rare that I have any visitors these days, so I welcome the company. It wasn't like that when we first moved here. Your Uncle and I used to host everyone in the neighborhood after the summer festival, and throughout the year. Our gatherings were the talk of the town."

"I've heard. Our Cousin Jolene was just talking about the summer festivals the other day. She and Mom had a lot to say about it."

He didn't seem to flinch when I mentioned Jolene or my mother. Instead, he led me around to his chicken coop and showed me a barn he built by hand. You could tell John was handy and spent a lot of time working with wood. The barn was filled with a lot of hand crafted bird houses, crates, and shelving.

"This looks like a pretty nice workshop." I perused around looking at all of his creations.

"Yep. I like to come out here and work on my hobby every once in a while. It gives me something to do."

John had enough wood carvings to open up a retail store. Some were painted and others were in their natural state. I could easily envision slapping little price tags on each one and selling it for a profit. I guess that was the businesswoman in me.

He seemed more like the type who might have a hard time parting ways with his work. He definitely wasn't the kind of guy I envisioned Mom having a fling with.

He took a few more puffs before throwing his cigarette on the ground and mashing it with his foot.

"Say, how's Jolene and your mother doing? I haven't seen them in ages."

"They're doing well."

"Is Jolene still crazier than ever?"

"Is she? From what I hear, she's gotten worse over the years."

He chuckled.

"She and your mother were the life of the party. They could light up a room. No matter where they went, they knew how to draw a crowd." He threw a stick toward the low hanging Spanish moss in his backyard.

"Yeah, according to Jolene, you and Mom used to have some good times together. She made it seem like you might know a lot about my family's history here in Savannah. She even hinted that you two may have been an item at some point."

He glanced over at me before lighting up another cigarette. We were outdoors in the Georgia heat. If I could barely breathe around him, I can only imagine what he was doing to his lungs with all those cigarettes.

"Ah, so that's why you came over here."

"I'm sorry?"

"You want to ask questions. You lawyer types are all the same. You have this roundabout way of trying to get information instead of just coming out and being direct. What do you want to know? I have nothing to hide."

He caught me off guard. I thought I was being rather subtle, but if he wanted direct, I was okay with that as well.

"John, I don't want to be disrespectful. But I believe you hold the keys to some information that my sisters and I deserve to know."

"Deserve? Ha, that's funny."

"You know what I mean. I don't believe in keeping secrets. Now that Jolene is back in our lives, she keeps sharing little tidbits of information here and there when she drinks. I just want to understand it, that's all. Everybody keeps bringing up the neighbor across the street. From what I gather, that would have to be you. You're the only one that's lived here for all these years."

"Well, I hate to burst your bubble, but if you think I had anything to do with your mother's past you're mistaken. I was a happily married man when I met your folks. We all were. Your Uncle Sammy, your parents, George and Jolene... all of us."

If that was the case, I don't know why Jolene was giving my mother such a hard time. And why Mom allowed her to. Or why mom had slipped up in the past and admitted some things that she wouldn't want most to know.

I immediately regretted bringing this up with John. I probably should've stuck to my primary purpose for coming here, which was to take care of the house and leave.

"I apologize. I suppose it was rather forward of me to come out and ask about such a thing to begin with. I probably should get going. Thank you for keeping an eye out on our place, John. We'll be around for another day and then we're heading back to Florida."

"There's no need to apologize," he said while exhaling smoke out of his nose.

I reached out and shook his hand before leaving to return across the street. The view of the house from John's yard looked like something straight out of an old classic movie. The porch fans were spinning and Ethan was pacing back and forth while talking on his cell phone. I thought about Payton's words as she pleaded with me not to get involved, then John called out to me.

"The person you really want to know about is my brother, Nathaniel. We call him Nate. He's the one who had eyes for Helen many years ago, even though he knew she was married."

I stopped in my tracks.

"Your brother? I don't understand."

"You wouldn't. You weren't even born yet. My brother was different from the rest of us. He was more like a well-polished rolling stone. He traveled around from state to state in a suit and called himself a businessman. None of us could ever really figure out what he did for a living. Whatever it was, he always managed to take care of himself. Whenever he'd come back to Savannah to visit, Momma would make such a fuss. That was her boy, no matter how old he was or what he did. She felt that way about all of us. He wasn't married and didn't have any plans to be. He used to always say he needed to get his business in order first and find a place to settle down. He said I was more of a family man than he was. I used to tease Nate about his way with the ladies. If you can imagine a tall handsome fella... with a clean hair cut... and his shoes always polished. These old country gals around here didn't know what to do with themselves. They'd all flock around him at the summer festival like he was a celebrity or something. Seemed like he always had them right in the palm of his hands. He was nothing but a wolf dressed in sheep's clothing as they say."

"He sounds like quite the character."

"He's a character alright. Or at least he was back then. Age has a funny way of catching up to you."

"If you don't mind me asking, what does this have to do with my mother?"

"One summer evening we were all hanging out here at that house playing music and having a good time. We had already spent the entire day together. The six of us, your uncle Samuel and the family. We should've been winding down for the evening but it seemed like with every passing hour and with every bottle of beer all we did was continue to hang out and party. We were so young back then. Most of us in our early twenties. What did we really know about being settled down? Your mother and Will, like myself, were just getting started with their lives. Martha and I just inherited this house from a family member who passed away. We felt so lucky, like we'd just hit the lotto. So, of course, we wanted to show off the new place and have our friends over."

He pointed toward a large area of his yard occupied by grass and a picnic table.

"Over there, we used to set up white lights around the perimeter of the yard and play music for dancing. Like I said. It was a good time to be had by all. Sadly, one evening we all pushed ourselves beyond our limits with the partying. My folks had already left for the evening, but my brother Nate was staying with us for a few days until his next trip. Your uncle left hours earlier, and your father was out cold in the living room. Seemed like the only ones left outside dancing and carrying on were Jolene, her husband George, Nate, and your mother."

As he spoke I imagined I was there standing by on the sidelines watching everything unfold.

"Everyone had been drinking heavily. I don't know exactly how Helen and Nate ended up together but one thing I'll never forget. When Will finally came around and went looking for Helen I don't think he was too happy with what he discovered. I heard a bunch of yelling and tussling going on out by the barn, and I knew whatever was going on couldn't be good. It took George and I both to get your father off Nate. By the time we finally did Nate took off like something was after him. He never bothered to hang around and explain his actions. He grabbed all his things from the house and left like something was after him. Things were different from that moment on. Everybody left to head back to Florida the next morning. That was the last summer we ever had everyone over at the house again. Nobody spoke a word about what happened that night. Everybody just went their separate ways."

"Did your brother ever tell you his version of what happened?"

"He never got into the details, but he said enough to let me know he wasn't an innocent party by any stretch of the imagination. That night was the perfect storm waiting to happen. Once Nate set his eyes on something he wanted he wasn't going to quit until he succeeded. He was used to having his way. That coupled with all the alcohol being served that night was a recipe for disaster. Your mother was a good woman. She was dedicated and loyal to Will and everyone knew it."

"Obviously not dedicated enough that she wouldn't act responsibly. She didn't have to drink. She could've just walked away and said we've had enough, let's go."

"Just live a little longer and you'll find out not everything in life is as easy as you make it out to be. Thankfully, Will felt differently about it. As a result, your parents went on to build a wonderful life together. They had their first baby girl later on that year and even started a business together. If Will would've viewed things the same way you do, you wouldn't be here today."

"Wait. This happened the same year Abby was born? And, how were you able to keep in touch with my parents to know how life turned out for them? Was it through Uncle Samuel?"

"Through your uncle and I also remained friends with your father. He used to return to Savannah every summer to visit and check on Samuel. Especially after your uncle's wife died. He stopped bringing Helen with him. He used to always say she was busy looking after the kids while taking care of things at the inn. But we had no reason to sever ties with each other. Your father knew that Nate's actions had nothing to do with me and our friendship."

"Man, now it makes sense why Dad used to come and visit Uncle Samuel on his own every year. Even I remember that much as a little girl. But you still haven't answered my question about Abby. If Mom and Dad had Abby later that year, who's to say that she's not Nate's child?"

"Ha! Does she look like the rest of you? Honestly, Rebecca, I think you're barking up the wrong tree with that one. If Abby belonged to anyone other than Will, I know your mother would've done the right thing and told us. I wouldn't go stirring up crazy ideas if I were you."

"Really? I'm not so sure about that. I only know as much as I do because of an accidental slip up and Cousin Jolene."

"That may be the case, but it's up to Helen and Will to decide how much they want to share. And, last I checked since they provided you with such a good life, it's up to you to decide not to judge them. Especially for something that happened so long ago."

I had so many questions running through my mind. None that would be resolved by talking to John any further, but at least I had a better idea of what Mom and Jolene were quarreling about when I went over to visit. The sound of footsteps crunching on the gravel behind me diverted my attention away from John.

"Everything alright over here? I was starting to wonder if you were coming back," Ethan said.

He reached out and hugged me around the waist.

"Everything is just fine. John was just giving me a tour of his property and sharing a little family history with me, that's all."

"Ah, that's nice. I'm sure you have stories to tell for days, John. Your land is absolutely breathtaking, by the way."

"Why, thank you, Ethan. It's rather peaceful here, if I say so myself."

"Tell me about it. Whenever we visit Savannah, it makes me consider moving. It might be nice if Rebecca and I could give John William a sweet little life here. We could even start our own law firm. It would be small at first, but I think we could make it work."

"Oh, really now? It sounds like you have everything all planned out." I gave Ethan a little shove. He knew I wasn't leaving Pelican Beach anytime soon, but it was a nice try.

"Maybe it's something to consider for the future. Who knows." Ethan smiled.

"Maybe. But, for now, let's head back over and see what kind of progress the contractors are making. John, again, thank you for everything. The management company has a few new prospects in place. They plan to have it rented out by the beginning of the new year. Keep your fingers crossed and please call us if you see anything that looks out of order."

"I sure will. It's been nice catching up with you, Miss Rebecca."

John reached out to shake hands and winked at us before walking back toward his home. The rest of our time was spent tying up loose ends with the rental. Every time I glanced across the street, I imagined a younger version of my parents, and what it must've been like the day Daddy made the discovery. The whole thing just made me angry. Thoughts lingered in the back of my mind about the timing of Abby's birth as well. Even though I'm sure John was right. If there was anything to know about Abby, I'm sure my parents would've told us by now. I get it that we all make mistakes. I just don't understand why my mother didn't trust me enough to tell me everything, instead of hushing me up like a little child.

"Cole, should I be nervous? We're down to six days left until Christmas and I feel like I'm having a hard time getting it together. If I'm not lying in bed, then I'm hugging the toilet. I still have a ton of wrapping to do, Natalie and I have to finish completing the markdowns at the store, there's so much that needs to be done."

"Payton, none of that matters if you're not feeling well. If I were you, I'd call Natalie and let her know you're going to need another day and ask her to cover the store. I can even stop by around lunch just to check on things if you want me to. As for the gifts, I'll work on that tonight after I get in. Your only priority is getting better. And, I think if you're still feeling under the weather later, you need to schedule an appointment to see the doctor first thing in the morning."

Cole brought a tray with hot tea and toast to the bed. He also brought a can of ginger ale and crackers since I'd been so indecisive lately. I sat up in bed wishing I had the energy to perform a simple task like getting up and brushing my teeth, making breakfast, or driving Emmie to school.

"If you could stop by and check on Natalie, that would be great. I'm sure I'll be fine by tomorrow. The Matthews girls weren't raised to go running to the doctor at the first sign of an ailment. I'll tough this one out just as I have in the past."

He shook his head and smiled.

"Alright, I will not tell you what to do but just remember, you're not a Matthews girl anymore. You're a Miller, and us Millers believe in going to the doctor if we're not better after a few days."

"Ha, yes, sir."

I watched Cole close the bedroom door behind him as he left for work. The morning shows were playing on the television, but I was having a hard time staying focused. I can't remember the last time I stayed home and watched television. My favorite shows were the ones that tuned in live from Times Square with all the latest holiday tips and recipes. I always had a dream that one Christmas I'd pack my bags and visit the big apple to see the Macy's Day parade. I don't know why I never did when I was living in Connecticut. Sometimes the best laid plans never come to fruition.

The dark overcast sky and tiny beads of water forming on the window was the perfect representation of how I was feeling on the inside. Thankfully, the phone rang, which served as a temporary distraction.

"Hello?"

"There you are. I just called the store and Natalie told me you were home sick today. What's the matter?"

"Abby, I feel awful. I don't know what's wrong with me but

it's been lingering for a couple of days, and it's driving me insane. I'm convinced I have a stomach virus."

"I'm sorry, Payton. Do you need me to bring you anything?"

"No. I'm going to try to tough it out. It can't last forever."

"When did you start feeling bad?"

"I've been feeling this way for the last four or five days off and on. I don't know."

"Well, let's just hope Emmie and Cole don't get it next."

"They couldn't be better. I'm the only one around here getting well acquainted with the porcelain around the toilet bowl."

"Ooh."

"Yeah. Exactly."

"Payton, I know it's been a while since we've had this discussion but... do you think you should take a pregnancy test just to rule out... you know..."

"The thought never crossed my mind. You know I can't have a baby. If pregnancy was in the cards, one would think that would've happened with Jack."

"Well... one would think, but that was a completely different time in your life. You were under a lot of stress because of all the challenges in your marriage. Things are different for you now. You're relaxed, you're happy, and you're in a loving relationship with somebody you trust."

"Yeah, but come on, Abby. It's not like my ovaries can just turn everything on like a light switch."

"Ha, you'd be surprised at what our bodies are capable of. Look, it was just a thought. If there's even the slightest chance you and Cole may have, you know... then you might want to take a test just to be certain."

"I see where you're going with this, Abby, but I still say there's no way. It's just a stomach bug. Really, I'll be fine. I promise."

"Okay. If you change your mind and you want me to swing by with a test, let me know."

"Thank you, but that won't be necessary."

"Okay. Hey, have you heard from Rebecca since she returned from her trip?"

"No. Not a peep. My head has been buried in the sand. You should reach out to her and see if there's anything we need to know before we all gather for Christmas dinner on Saturday."

"I thought you didn't want her to go poking around behind Mom's back."

"I don't. I also know my little sister well enough to know she probably did the opposite. I just want to make sure if there are any fires to put out we get it done ahead of time so we can all enjoy a peaceful dinner."

"True. Alright, I'll call her this afternoon. In the meantime, text me if you need anything."

"Thanks, Abby."

"Bye."

A pregnancy test? Nah. There's no way. In the beginning, my ex-husband Jack and I wanted a baby so badly we would've given anything to have one. We tried for a long time until it became obvious my body wasn't able to produce children. The doctor never confirmed it or anything, but it didn't take a rocket scientist to figure out what we were doing wasn't working. It was around that time that Jack's attention shifted on to other things. Late nights, job functions, and everything else except for our marriage. At that point having a baby fell way to the bottom of our to do list. Things became so bad in our marriage that it was no longer a point of conversation. As it turned out, it was probably the best thing that could've ever happened.

~

I awoke to the sound of the house alarm announcing the front door was open. I knew it was Cole just by the way he punched in the alarm code and tossed his keys in the basket. The red numbers on my digital clock read 2:45. I'm not sure how the day got away from me, but apparently I needed the sleep. While still struggling to fully wake up, the bedroom door creaked open and Emmie's thin frame stood towering over me.

"Are you feeling better?" she asked.

I removed my hair out of my face and rolled over.

"I think so. How was your day, love?"

"Not that great." A tear fell down her cheek, but she quickly wiped it away.

"I'm so sorry, Emms. What happened?"

"Some kids in my science class were making fun of me for knowing all the answers to the questions. They kept whispering things like teacher's pet and calling me names."

"Did you say something to the teacher?"

"No. It would only make things worse. If they get in trouble, then I'll get teased even more whenever the teacher is not around. It's not a big deal. I'm just mad and wish they would leave me alone."

"I'll march right in that school and see that they never bother you again. Who is it? Give me their names."

"No. You can't. Everyone at school will laugh at me."

Cole peeked his head in the door. Emmie immediately changed her demeanor, as if she didn't want Cole to know.

"How's my sick patient doing?" he asked.

"Much better."

"Are you sure? You're in the same spot that I left you in this morning."

"I know. Looks like I needed the extra rest. Now, my only challenge will be getting back to sleep tonight."

"I'll bet."

"Emmie and I were just talking about..."

Emmie cleared her throat loudly and gave me an awkward look. Since she was sitting at my bedside with her back facing Cole, he didn't seem to notice.

"What was that?" Cole called from across the room.

"Umm, Emmie and I were just catching up. I was asking her about the school day."

"Oh, alright. You two catch up while I head downstairs and make you a bowl of soup."

"Thank you."

Once the coast was clear, I turned to Emmie and waited for an explanation.

"I don't want Dad to know. The last time I told him something like this, he showed up at school. I'm in sixth grade now. The kids will make fun of me and torture me if my Dad shows up to school."

"How about we make a deal? Your dad has a right to know, sweetheart. He just wants to protect you. I have an idea. How about we come up with a plan that doesn't involve one of us showing up at school or embarrassing you? We can include your dad and brainstorm a few ideas as a team. How does that sound?"

"Good, I guess."

"You guess? You guess! Come on, where's that big smile of yours that lights up a room?"

I cherished these moments and wanted to do everything I could to make Emmie feel welcomed to confide in me. Not only because I was her step-mother, but because I knew she was at a stage where everything in her world was changing.

Later that evening, I messaged Abby to call me.

"Hello?"

"Hey, Payton. I got your message. Are you sure you want to do this? You didn't sound too convinced earlier today."

"I'm still not convinced. But the nausea is lingering off and on, and you planted the seed in my head. Now I'm wondering if I should do it to completely rule out pregnancy altogether."

"Did you tell Cole?"

"Goodness, no. I know he would be over the moon, but he also knows the chances are very unlikely. I don't see any point in getting his hopes up. Besides, I feel like such a hypocrite tonight. I had a long talk with Emmie about the importance of sharing an incident that happened at school with Cole. Now, look at me. I can't even tell my own husband that I'm thinking about taking a pregnancy test."

"Why can't you? What's the big deal? I'm happy to pick one up for you, but I think Cole would be even happier to be involved, don't you think?"

"If the test is negative, which I'm sure it is, I don't want him to be disappointed."

"I think he can handle it, Payton. But if you want, I can swing by the pharmacy and be over there within an hour."

"An hour?"

"Yes, if that works for you."

"I have to come up with an excuse or something."

"Say that I'm stopping by to visit and see how you're feeling. That wouldn't be out of the ordinary, would it?"

"Abby, how often to you drop everything and leave the kids and Wyatt at eight o'clock at night?"

"Alright, how about you make up something about a few gifts that I have to drop off. That way no one can ask you questions because they'll assume it's a surprise for Christmas."

"Again, it's eight o'clock, remember?"

"Okay, I don't know what to tell you. Maybe you should just put the whole idea out of your head for now and revisit this tomorrow. Are you going to the store in the morning?"

"I have no choice. I've been out of it for the last couple days."

"Okay, then tomorrow it is. I'll meet you at the store for lunch."

"I don't know if it's a good idea to do this around Natalie."

"Look. It's not like you're inviting her in the bathroom and asking you to read the test."

"No, but it could alter my mood for the rest of the day based on whatever the reading says."

"I thought you were confident about what the results would be?"

"I was. I mean, I am. Argh, Abby, you're driving me nuts."

"Okay. How about I meet you at the end of the day. That way you'll have all the privacy in the world and can react however you want without concern about who's around."

"That sounds better."

She sighed on the other end of the line.

"Good. I'll see you tomorrow. I'm going to go take a couple of aspirin."

"Hush, Abby! I'm the one who needs an aspirin." I laughed.

"You need something, alright."

"Thank you for doing this for me. I'll see you tomorrow."

"Love you, Sis," she said.

"Love you, too. Bye."

JOLENE

"Helen, let me look at this grocery list of yours and see if anything needs to be added for Christmas dinner. Christmas isn't right if you don't have certain items on the table."

"Like what? I have all of our family favorites on that list. I haven't overlooked a thing. I know it like the back of my hand."

"I'm sure you do, but it never hurts to have an extra pair of eyes. Let's see what we have here. Mashed potatoes, edamame, turkey. Turkey? Didn't everybody have enough turkey for Thanksgiving? How about the pot roast? Surely pot roast is an option at the table along with a maple glazed ham. You can't forget the maple glazed ham with lightly roasted pineapples to decorate the outside. Mmm, my mouth is watering up just thinking about it. We always switched things up for the holidays. One year I went with a Texas barbecue theme. Folks raved about that just as much as they did about the glazed ham."

"Jolene, who's going to make all of that? The kids enjoy having another turkey along with a prime roast for dinner. No one has ever complained about it before."

"Maybe it's time to shake things up a bit. Nobody wants to eat from the same old tired menu year after year."

"Tired menu? There's nothing tired about my menu. It's a thoughtful, well planned out menu filled with family traditions."

"Really? Well, even traditions can get tired. Where's the succotash?"

"Succotash? For Christmas? Jolene, you must be kidding me. I think you need to focus on something else and let the real chef take care of the menu."

"Is that so? You must think the only thing I'm good for is taking care of the sick. I know how to cook, you know. And, I know how to plan an appetizing meal that will keep folks coming back for more. George and I used to host our neighbors and friends over at the house all the time."

"I'm sure you did, Jolene. But my family is expecting a holiday dinner, not something fit for a pig pen."

"A pig pen? That's rather harsh, Helen. But instead of me arguing with you, I have an idea."

"I'm listening."

"Why don't we put our skills to the test? Prepare your old washed up menu since it's a family tradition. I will prepare a few dishes of my own and put it out among the other food. Then, afterward, we can sit back and let the family decide what they like best."

"A contest, Jolene? What are you, a child?"

"No, I'm not a child, but I'm confident about my cooking and I believe I just made you nervous about yours. I think you're afraid Cousin Jolene may put your Christmas cooking to shame."

"Ha! Not a chance. Your best dish couldn't entice my family away from their mother's cooking no matter how hard you try."

"Well, if you're so confident, then accept the challenge."

Helen snatched the list away and put it in the front pocket of her apron.

"Fine," she said.

"Good. I think I'll add a dessert as well. My rum cake is to die for."

"Go figure," Helen murmured under her breath.

"What was that?"

"Nothing."

"Mmm hmm. Well, it looks like I have my work cut out for me. I don't normally wait until the eleventh hour to plan these sorts of things, so I better get to it. Oh, and before I forget, if it's alright with you, I'm going to spend a couple of hours out of the house this afternoon. I figured I'd treat myself to lunch and pick up a last-minute gift or two."

"It's fine by me. We'll be here when you get back."

"Good. I'll head upstairs and check on William, work on this list, and leave within the hour."

Helen stood back and watched as I left the kitchen. She didn't have to admit it, but I knew she was worried about being outshined at her own holiday gathering.

The Inn at Pelican Beach had become my secret getaway when I needed a breath of fresh air. Things had changed over the years, but I hadn't seen the place in over fifteen years, so it was to be expected. There was this little bar area off the veranda that was the perfect spot for people watching while I ordered a drink.

"Miss Jolene, how can I serve you today?"

"Frank, please call me Jolene. I'll take my usual. Be sure to make it on the rocks for me, okay?"

"Sure thing. It looks like you're toting quite a few shopping bags today. Squeezing in some last-minute shopping?"

"Eh, I picked up an item or two, but I'm finished mostly. I'm not one for holiday crowds, if you know what I mean."

"I certainly do. It's not that bad around here, though. The beauty about Pelican Beach is the peace that settles over the community every evening between six and seven. Have you noticed it since you've been here? All the shops close and everyone makes it home around the same time to have dinner with their families. It's a beautiful thing. Nothing like what you would experience living in a big city."

"I have noticed that. It is rather peaceful, but nothing compares to back home. Beach life is pleasant and all, but I miss the marshland and the backwoods where I could fire off a couple rounds for relaxation."

"Ha! Jolene, you should've said something. I can point you toward the nearest fire range, if you want me to."

"Range? No way. You're talking to a country girl at heart. The best shooting range is in the great outdoors."

"Where did you say you were from again?"

"I didn't say. I rarely go around telling my business to strangers."

Just then a handsome fella emerged from the back room.

CHRISTMAS AT PELICAN BEACH

He approached Frank from behind and gave him a pat on the shoulder.

"You're doing a mighty fine job back here, Frank. Everything looks wonderful. I just went through the inventory and I couldn't be more pleased."

"Thank you, sir."

The gentleman looked over and tipped his hat off to me.

"Howdy, ma'am. Can I get you a refill?"

"Normally I'd love to, but I have to get going soon."

"That's too bad. Is this your first time visiting the inn? Seems like I've seen you around before. A pretty woman like yourself would be hard to miss."

"Aren't you a flirt?" I smiled.

"You may have seen me once or twice. I spent most of my days here back in the eighties. I highly doubt you were here back then."

Frank, the bartender, flipped a rag over his shoulder and leaned on the counter to listen in. However, the gentleman waited until Frank found something else to do before he continued to speak.

"The eighties? No, I wasn't even in the hospitality business back then."

He extended his hand across the bar.

"I'm David, by the way. It's nice to meet you."

"Likewise, I'm Jolene. So, what do you do around here besides making sure the bar stays fully stocked?"

Frank chuckled from the other side of the bar.

"Let's see. Every once in a while I poke my nose down in the kitchen to make sure we're cooking up food that keeps the guests happy. Then they also have me checking up on guests' services and the finance department. You know, the usual stuff that comes along with working at an inn."

"Good grief! You'd think the owner would have a hand in some of that instead of leaving it all to their staff. That's the problem these days. Local businesses aren't like they used to be at all. Back in the day, you could walk into a mom and pop store and meet the owners first hand. Nowadays, people are too busy to get involved. I'm sorry you have to deal with all that. Things sure have changed around here."

I took my last sip and put my hand up for Frank to refill my glass. I was enjoying the company and decided to extend my visit a little while longer.

"Have things really changed that drastically here at the inn? You know, since you last visited. Assuming that you remember what the service was like and all," he asked.

"I've only been back about five or six months. But just from a few visits, I know one thing that's missing is the owner. I haven't met the bum once. So much for a small town experience. What good are all the renovations and upgrades if you're not here to meet the customers? It's an inn, for goodness sake. Frank here has been very accommodating and friendly. Maybe he should own the place. Isn't that right, Frank?"

"Oh, no. Not me, Miss Jolene. I wouldn't know the first thing about running an inn, but I know how to mix a good cocktail for you."

David folded his arms and stood there with a smile that revealed his dimples. He had a full faced beard but through all the hair, if I had to guess, he looked to be a few years younger than me. Something about him reminded me of my George with his raspy voice.

"Besides, Miss Jolene, what this nice fellow failed to

mention the whole time he's been talking to you is he is the owner. You are getting what you call a small town experience right now as we speak," Frank said.

"Now, why'd you go and do that for? I was having fun with her until you went and spoiled it. That's going to cost you, Frank." He teased.

Frank pointed at David.

"I'm going to repeat what you always tell the staff 'customer service always comes first'." Miss Jolene here deserved to know the truth."

"Yeah, yeah, yeah. Go on and help those customers over there, Mr. Customer Service."

David wiped down the counter space near where I was sitting and laid out a snack bowl filled with nuts.

"So, you're the owner. You let me sit here and talk trash about you this whole time and didn't say a word."

"My apologies. I was just having a little fun with you. I had every intention of telling you who I was in just a little while."

"Mmm hmm. You've done a nice job with the place, but it's starting to have a bit of a hotel chain vibe to it. Small town beach communities and big chains don't mix. Other than that, I like it. Keep up the good work."

"Why, thank you, I'm glad you approve. I thought the place needed a little updating when I took over last year. All of my locations have undergone renovations at some point. You have to be able to keep up with the demands of the times we're living in."

"Did you say all of your locations?"

"Yes, ma'am."

"How many locations do you have? I can't imagine being able to keep up with more than one inn."

"Ha. I'm a businessman. That's what I do. This would be my fifth location. I was looking into one other place for a while, but the asking price was a little steep for my pockets."

"Interesting. I don't see how you keep up with it myself."

"I have a staff that helps me keep up with it, that's how. I personally interviewed each one of my staff members and put them through state-of-the-art training. I have the revenue to show for it. If you provide your customers with a great experience, they'll come back for more."

"I guess. Hey, you figured out a plan that works for you. That's the whole point of going into business in the first place, right?"

"You guess? Assuming you have some experience with owning a business, how would you have done it?"

"For starters, I wouldn't own an establishment like this because I can only handle being around a lot of people in small doses. After a while, somebody is bound to get on my nerves and drive me to drink."

"Ha! You look like you're doing a fine job with that one all by yourself."

I cut him a fierce look which made him quickly retract his statement.

"I'm sorry. Please continue."

"As I was saying... I wouldn't run a place like this. I'd rather have time to be out in nature, shooting targets, or fishing or doing something relaxing."

"I'm surprised. I would've never guessed that a beautiful woman like yourself would enjoy shooting targets."

"Yeah, well, never judge a book by its cover. I know how to carry myself like a lady and whip your bottom in just about any sport imaginable. Especially target shooting."

"Sassy! I like it. Tell me more."

"There's not much more to tell. I'm not to be mistaken for all beauty and no brains, that's all. You, on the other hand, never finished telling me about this state-of-the-art staff training of yours."

"What about it?"

"Do you really think that's the best way to go about running an inn? Nothing can replace you as the owner living here and knowing the locals first hand."

"What's it with you and all the personalized thinking? Look around this place. Everyone is eating, drinking, and being merry. Guests are checking in and out regularly. I see nothing wrong with the business as is."

"You wouldn't see it if it hit you with a brick. You're too much of a big time, city slicker type. My cousin used to have this place packed to the gills, and everybody knew each other by name. There's a holiday festival this year. Did you volunteer the inn to take part or donate to show your support? When is the last time you hosted an event here for the community? The Matthews used to host an annual Luau night. What kind of events do you host?"

"Oh, I see. So, that's what this is about. You're related to the Matthews, and they sent you here to spy on me and offer your opinion about how things are going since I took over."

"That couldn't be farther from the truth."

"Sure sounds like it to me. Why else would you be so passionate about the inn?"

"Look. I'm related to them, but the whole idea that they sent me over here couldn't be farther from the truth. I came here so I could get a break and enjoy some time by myself. As for your business, you asked how would I run things and so I told you. Period. Don't go getting your britches in a bunch with me."

He stared at me for a moment and started to laugh so hard he nearly drew everyone's attention over to the bar.

"What's so funny?"

He continued to laugh.

"Woman. You are so funny! I don't think I've ever met anybody like you before. You just come right in here and start firing off like a pistol. I've never seen anything like it."

"I fire off more like an AR-15, not a pistol."

"Yep, that, too."

He stood there and laughed till his eyes were filled with tears. I didn't know whether to join in or be offended.

"I'm so glad I could provide you with entertainment, Mr. David. I guess this is my cue to be on my way. I still have to visit the grocery store before heading back to the house."

"Oh, come on, now. Don't leave. I didn't mean to upset you."

"I'm not upset. I have thick skin, so there's very little that you could do or say to hurt me."

"Well, that's good to know because I really am enjoying your company and would hate for you to leave on my account."

"I'm not leaving on your account. I really do have an important trip to make to the grocery store before it gets too late. My cousin's wife seems to think she's the only one who can cook a good Christmas dinner, and I'm determined to prove her wrong."

"So you're having a cook off?"

"Something like it."

"What are you going to make?"

"Wouldn't you like to know? I can't give away my secrets."

"It's not like I'm going to be there. Who am I going to tell? The only thing I have going on for Christmas is sitting here at the inn for another week until it's time to leave."

"Surely, you're going to spend Christmas with your family?"

"I hadn't planned on it. I'm a loner, Jolene. I'm too busy traveling from one business to the next to have time for sentimental holidays."

"That's too bad. You can have all the money in the world, but if you're lonely and have no one to share it with, what good will it do you, anyway?"

"I guess."

"I know. All the things I thought mattered didn't mean a hill of beans when my George passed away. I've been alone ever since and would give anything to bring him back. Priorities, David. You gotta have your priorities in order. I tell you what. Even if only for a couple of hours, you need to stop by the cottage and have Christmas dinner with us."

"With the Matthews? No, no, Jolene. It's nice of you to think of me, but I don't think that's a good idea. Lady Matthews and her daughter weren't too thrilled about my way of doing business when I bought the place from them. I can't imagine that would be a good idea."

"Nonsense, Helen and Will have an open door policy to all. The more the merrier is Helen's famous line. Plus, I'll need somebody who will give an honest opinion about my cooking. Bring Frank with you if he doesn't have any plans."

"Jolene, I really don't think..."

"I won't take no for an answer. If you come at least, I'll have someone interesting to talk to. Here's the address. Don't lose it."

I slipped a napkin across the counter with the address to the cottage and the time he should be there.

"Oh, and I'm sure you can spare a bottle of wine or two from your stock room back there. You know what they say, never show up to a party empty-handed."

"Alright, Miss Jolene. But if your family gets upset, I'm going to tell them it's your fault."

"It wouldn't be the first time I upset them about something, and it probably won't be the last. I'll see you in a couple of days."

ABBY

"Abby, I just heard the bells ringing up front. I thought you locked the door before we came back here."

"I could've sworn I turned the lock."

"It's been acting up lately. I need to get it fixed."

"Alright, you stay in there and follow the next step in the directions. I'll be right back."

No sooner than I turned the corner did I bump right into my younger sister Rebecca who was holding my nephew in her arms. I could already see this was heading downhill before we started. I had Payton in the bathroom trying to take a pregnancy test, and Rebecca who was nosey and would probably turn around and tell if she found out what was going on.

"Hey, Abby. I thought that was your SUV out front. John William, say hi to your Aunt Abby."

I smothered his plump little cheeks with kisses before continuing the conversation.

"Yep, that's me. Guess it's kind of hard to hide a big old Chevy."

"Why would you try to hide?"

"I'm not trying to hide. I just meant if I were ever trying to hide, it would be hard to do because the truck is so big."

"Right. Where's Payton?"

"She's in the bathroom. I'm sure she'll be out soon. How was your trip to Savannah?"

"It was productive. We were able to get a lot accomplished."

"Including talking to the neighbor across the street?"

"Maybe."

"What's that supposed to mean?"

Before she could respond Payton yelled from the back.

"Abby, is everything alright?"

"Yes, everything is fine, I'll be right there."

"Alright, I need you to come back and help me read this thing. I can't tell what this is supposed to say."

"Hold on, Payton. I'll be right there."

Rebecca looked beyond where I was standing toward the back of the store.

"Why don't we just go back there so you can help her out."

"Oh, I will. But first why don't you explain what you meant by maybe? You either spoke to the neighbor across the street, or you didn't. It's not that complicated."

"I'm not talking about this in front of John William."

"Really, Rebecca? He's a baby."

"So, you think he doesn't recognize when his mother is upset about something?"

"I think he recognizes when his mother is acting like a drama queen."

Payton bellowed out from the back of the store again.

"Abby, what's taking you so long? I can't tell if this stupid test is negative, positive, or what."

Rebecca's eyes widened.

"Is she taking a pregnancy test?"

Oh, goodness. I was trying my best but if Payton was going to keep broadcasting her business for everyone out front to hear, then I didn't know what else I could do.

"I'll be right back," I said.

"So what am I, chopped liver? I guess you two were going to team up on this one and leave me in the dark, as usual."

"Rebecca, why do you always find a way to make everything about yourself? I said I'll be right back, now hang on a moment."

I turned to see Payton standing at the threshold of the break room. She held the face of the stick so that we could see the results on the screen.

"I told you I wasn't pregnant. The negative line is showing up the strongest. The other line is so faint, I don't think it counts."

"Let me see it. Maybe there's some sort of mistake."

My assessment of the results was the same as Payton's. There was a faint plus sign in the background while the negative appeared the strongest. I remembered the first time I ever used one of these tests was right before I found out I was pregnant with Maggie. I also remembered the feeling that came along with all of my negative tests and it made me feel a little melancholy for Payton.

"Not that you two care what I think, but I'd get a second opinion if I were you. I was confident that my first test was negative, only to find out that I was expecting John William several weeks later," Rebecca said as she put him down to explore around the store.

"It's not a big deal. I'm sure the results are correct. We all know that my womb is not fit for carrying babies anyway."

"Payton, don't say that. You've never known that to be the case. You've always assumed. With all the advanced technology out there, I don't see why you couldn't have a child of your own. You'll never know unless you sit down with the doctors and get their take on it," I said.

It bothered me that she was so quick to give up. I always thought Payton would make a great mother if given the chance.

"Abby, I'm forty-three years old. I hadn't exactly planned on starting the journey into motherhood at my age. This is something I would've preferred tackling years ago. And before you start, I know women have children in their forties all the time. I get it. But, clearly that plan isn't for me. So, let's just drop it. I thank you for coming over here and showing support, but I'm not going to the doctor to sit down and talk about advanced technology or anything else for that matter."

"Not even your stomach bug? You could at least try and get to the bottom of why you've been so sick lately."

"I'll figure it out." Payton turned to John William.

"Hi, sweet boy, how's my handsome nephew doing?"

He continued to wobble around the store while touching everything in sight.

"Well, it looks like I stopped by at the wrong time. I thought I'd say hello and ask what you planned to bring to Mom's house for dinner. I didn't realize I would be interrupting you," Rebecca said.

"You're not interrupting, Rebecca. I haven't been feeling good this week so we just wanted to rule out the idea that I could be pregnant. It's nothing, really. As for the food, why don't you just give Mom a call and ask?"

"Mmm." Rebecca seemed to brush off the idea and followed my nephew instead.

"You don't sound so enthusiastic. Have you spoken to Mom since you've been back?" Payton asked.

"No, I had to hit the ground running when we returned. I haven't had time."

Payton looked at her but didn't say a word. I, on the other hand, could quickly read between the lines. Rebecca was trying to act nonchalant but I think we both knew better. She definitely had a chip on her shoulder about something.

"Why are the two of you looking at me like that?" Rebecca snarled.

"Don't look at me. You're the one who left for Savannah with a chip on your shoulder and returned with one. I don't know what kind of bug you got up your butt, but hopefully you lose the attitude so we can all enjoy Christmas together."

"Whatever, Abby."

"Don't whatever Abby, me. I'm serious. This should be a special Christmas for Mom and Dad. For all of us, but especially for them. Things are changing before our very eyes. They're getting older now. We don't how much longer we'll have to enjoy Christmases hosted by our parents at the cottage."

"Abby's right, Rebecca. Whatever is bothering you, the best thing to do is let it out now so we can get past it already."

"Some things aren't so easy to get over."

"Does this have anything to do with you talking to Uncle Samuel's neighbor?" Payton asked.

"Oh no you don't. You two aren't pressing me about

anything that may have taken place since we met for dinner. I confided in you at the inn and you both treated me like a little child. You totally disregarded what I had to say, just like Mom totally disregards everything I have to say. I'm sick and tired of it. This topic is off limits as far as I'm concerned."

While Payton was trying to be diplomatic, I was having visions of wrapping my hands around Rebecca's throat. Thankfully, for her, our mother raised me to be a lady.

"So that's what this is about? Somebody hurt your feelings, so now you're going to pout and act like a little brat?" Rebecca looked at me with widened eyes.

"You know what, Abby? I thought you and I had turned a corner together. Right after I had John William I thought you and I were starting to bond. But, I see nothing has changed. As far as I'm concerned, you guys can go ahead and have Christmas dinner without me. Since I'm not appreciated, I'm sure I won't be missed, anyway. I'm sure Ethan's mother would be happy to have us come to her house, instead."

"Don't... you... dare." Payton looked as if she was about to grow horns.

"Excuse me?"

"You heard me, Rebecca. Don't you dare be so selfish as to ruin Christmas for everyone. Despite all this nonsense you're talking as of late, Mom would be devastated if you weren't there and you know it."

Rebecca stood tight lipped with her chin up. I was surprised to see her at a loss for words. She usually had a way of trying to make sense out of things that really made no sense at all. This time Payton called her bluff.

~

Wyatt could tell I was irritated later that evening. It was probably the sound of the dishes clanging as I emptied the dishwasher, that gave him a clue. He offered to prepare dinner for me and the kids, and since it was a rare occasion I didn't refuse. Besides, how difficult was it to heat up leftovers in the microwave?

"Are you okay, honey? You don't seem like yourself tonight."

"I'm fine. Just irritated at Rebecca, that's all."

"Oh, goodness. What now?" he asked with a slight close lipped smile.

"She's just being her usual self. You know, the queen of self-centeredness. Except the only problem is, this time it could actually have a negative impact on Christmas," I whispered, not wanting the kids to overhear.

"Christmas. Really? Do you think she'd take it that far? I don't understand what it is with you three. You've always had such a love hate relationship with Rebecca. You would think at some point you'd outgrow all the nonsense."

"You three? Payton and I can't take responsibility for her actions."

"No, you can't, but you don't have to fan the flames either. When she starts, you and Payton have to learn to walk away."

I fixed my gaze on Wyatt. He was about one minute from getting evicted and sent to the dog house for the night.

"So, I guess I'm not supposed to defend myself or ever speak up for what's right?"

"No, honey, that's not what I'm saying."

"Don't you honey me, Wyatt. You know I'm a straight shooter. Tell me how you really feel."

He hesitated.

"Aw, Abby, come on. Don't turn this on me. I didn't do anything except heat up the dinner and try to make you feel better."

I took a deep breath and moved a little closer to stroke his beard.

"You're right, Wyatt. You did make the evening special. Thank you."

"You know what else would make the evening special?"

"Don't push your luck, buddy. We've gotta see to it that the kids adhere to their bedtime so we can start part one of gift wrapping tonight."

"Not again. Why do we have to go through this every year? Seriously, Abby, all the gift buying is getting out of control. The kids are getting older now. I'm sure they'll understand if Santa has to leave them their top favorite items instead of buying a ton of junk they don't need. Where's the gifts from last year? I'm sure half of the items were forgotten about."

"Christmas only comes once a year, Wyatt. If you're getting cranky over gift wrapping, I think you'll survive."

"It's not just the gift wrapping, Abby. It's the expense of it all. Maggie's not even into Santa anymore."

"So, what does that mean? Should we tell her sorry, the gifts stop when you stop believing?"

"No, of course not. But we could start setting a new example around this house and stop being so wasteful, that's all."

I let out a long exhale.

"Forget I said anything. We'll get through it like we always do."

Wyatt tossed the dish rag into the sink and started rummaging through the refrigerator.

"Am I missing something here? We went from having a nice dinner, to me telling you about Rebecca, to this. What do you mean 'we'll get through it like we always do'? If the gift wrapping really bothers you that much, I'll figure out another plan. Maybe I can pay for a gift wrapping service in town. No big deal."

Wyatt popped open a can of soda and took a few gulps.

"It is a big deal, Abby. I wasn't going to tell you like this. I was going to wait until after Christmas, but the truth is we can't afford any of it."

"What do you mean?"

"I've barely been able to put a dent in any of our debt. I still have outstanding loans from law school that should've been paid off ages ago. Then there's our credit card debt, the mortgage on our dream house, and let's not forget the BMW and the double XL sized SUV in the driveway. Things are starting to burst at the seams, Abby. Maybe if we had more than one income it would work, but I can't shoulder this on my own for much longer."

"Whoa. I certainly didn't see this coming."

"I don't know how you didn't see it coming. I've never hidden our finances from you."

I felt a rush come over me that caused tears to well up in my eyes.

"Yeah, but you know I don't pay attention to the details. I've always left that up to you and just assumed everything was under control."

"Well, then, let me be the first to say that everything is not under control. Our consumer debt is through the roof right now and if we don't start making some serious changes, we're going to find ourselves in a really bad place."

"I really wish you would've said something long before now."

"I'm sorry, Abby. I've always wanted to support you and give you whatever made you happy. Even now I hate that I'm having to say anything at all. I've always wanted to be the husband who could just take care of everything but that only works when you're not spending beyond your means."

A tear ran down the side of my cheek.

"So, how much debt are we talking about?"

"We're at the six figure mark."

"That's another mini mortgage," I said with a sarcastic chuckle.

"Yep, something like it. Plus, the firm is cutting back with our usual bonuses this year, so..."

"Well, I feel like I just got the wind knocked out of me. But, the one thing I know for sure is you didn't marry a quitter. We got ourselves into this mess and we'll get ourselves out of it."

"Really?"

"Really!"

He looked at me in disbelief.

"That's definitely the Christmas spirit. I appreciate the support, hun, but you do realize that having six figure debt is going to require a lot of sacrifice, right?"

"Well, let's just buckle down and make a plan. I married you for better or worse, Wyatt. I may need to shed a few more tears later on when you're not looking, in the closet, with a glass of wine. But we'll get through this. We're a team, we can do this."

He held his head back and let out a hardy laugh.

"Not the closet, Abby. Anywhere but the closet."

"Hey, sometimes I need to hide when the kids are driving me crazy. What can I say?"

"Alright, I'll give you that. But, seriously, thank you for being so supportive, babe."

"Oh, when this is all over you're going to pay me back with a nice vacation or something. Paid with cash, of course. In the meantime, I think we need to get creative to help reduce some of these bills."

"I'm open for ideas."

"I overheard one of the talk shows the other day on satellite radio about this very topic. People were calling in talking about how much debt they paid off. It wouldn't hurt to use a few ideas from the show. For starters, we could cancel all of our memberships until we get back on our feet again."

"True."

"Some of the other ideas were a bit extreme but, Wyatt, I'll do whatever it takes to help us get out of this mess. I've never been the stuck up type who thinks it's beneath me to get job."

"But, what about the kids? It's always been our dream for you to stay home with them."

"Maybe I can find something that works with their school schedule. I don't know, maybe I can even apply for a position at the school. It's been a while, but I'm sure my degree in education can be put to use in some capacity."

"What will your PTA friends think?"

"Wyatt, I thought you knew me better than that. I couldn't care less about what the white jean brigade has to say."

"Ha, you probably would put them in their place and not even flinch."

"Now we're talking."

Wyatt placed both his hands on my face and drew me in for a sweet kiss.

"I honestly feel like the luckiest guy on the planet. You don't know how much it means to me to have your support, Abby. I love you."

"I love you, too."

I turned him around and whacked him on the fanny with a dish cloth. It was the perfect time to let my playful side emerge to keep from shedding additional tears. I knew the road ahead wasn't going to be easy, but we would get through it, together, as we always have in the past.

PAYTON

"$\mathcal{H}$i, Payton."

"Natalie, I was just about to call you. It's not like you to be late. Is everything okay?"

"Not really. I mean. I'm fine, but I won't be able to come to the store for a while."

"What's wrong?"

Natalie burst into a heart wrenching sob. Immediately my thoughts went to her mother, but I waited for confirmation first.

"She didn't make it," she barely whispered.

"No. Aww, Natalie. I'm so sorry, love. Are you at the house? I can close the store down and come be with you right now."

"I'm still at the hospital. My aunt flew in from Texas yesterday, so I'm not alone."

"I wasn't aware that your mom was in the hospital. I'm glad your aunt is there with you, but please know that I'm here to help in any way I can. Seriously."

"Thank you, Payton. I didn't want to say anything because I know you haven't been feeling well. Honestly, I thought it was going to be another one of her brief visits to the hospital. I had no idea..."

Her voice trailed off for a moment.

"I guess it really doesn't matter now, but Mom was so thankful for your invitation to Christmas dinner. I believe she would've tried with all her might to make it if she had the strength. She always appreciated the way you looked out for me and gave me a full-time job. Mom always referred to you as my miracle boss." Natalie laughed in between the sniffles.

"I don't know about the miracle part, I just saw your potential. She raised you to be a beautiful young lady on the inside and out. You know the invitation still stands if you and your aunt don't want to be alone for Christmas. Of course, we'd all understand either way."

"Thanks. It's likely that I won't make it. Maybe next year."

"Absolutely. Take as much time as you need. And do not hesitate to call me for anything, anytime, day or night, you hear?"

"Yes. Thank you, Payton."

A teardrop fell on the countertop as I hung up the phone. It made little sense to me that a young girl like Natalie was stripped of so much at such a young age. Since we met, I watched her lose everything from her friendships, her boyfriend, her degree, living a normal life, and now the most precious of them all, her mother. Moments like this made me question God's motive, but ultimately, I knew he had a plan greater than I could comprehend.

I diverted my attention to the sound of carolers singing across the street. It was an uplifting reminder that my family had so much to be thankful for this holiday season. The phone ringing interrupted the sweet melody.

"Picture Perfect, how can I help you?" I answered.

"Hello, may I speak to Payton Miller, please."

"Speaking."

"Hi, this is Karen from the Pelican Beach Medical Center. We received your message about coming in to see Dr. Marx."

"Yes, thanks for calling back. I realize it's probably too late to get an appointment this week, but I was wondering if you had an opening for after Christmas?"

"Actually, you're in luck. We had a cancellation for tomorrow morning at ten if you're available."

"You're taking appointments on Christmas Eve?"

"We are until noon."

"I wasn't expecting to get in so soon, but sure, I'll take it."

"Wonderful. Now, I just have to record what you're coming in for and you'll be all set."

"Uh, well. I guess you could say I've had a stomach bug for several days now. Not really sure what it is, actually."

"Uh, huh. Do you still have an appetite?"

"At times, yes. And, at other times, I'm just as nauseous as I can be. And, ma'am, I should probably request a pregnancy test. You know, just to be certain."

"I understand. We'll give you the works and hopefully help you feel better in time for Christmas. Alright, I have you down for ten o'clock tomorrow. Has anything changed with your insurance?"

"No, everything's the same."

"Great, we'll see you in the morning."

"Thank you. See you then."

~

Emmie and I spent the evening arranging several gift bags filled with Christmas cookies. She came up with the idea of delivering a batch to the local nursing home and another batch to the children's hospital. She had a heart of gold and always challenged me to be a better person. I love that about her. Emmie's kind heart, sense of selflessness, beauty, and wit were all attractive traits that would carry her far in life. Sometimes I quietly watched and envisioned what the older version of Emmie would be like. She'd probably be the class valedictorian and the driving force behind her college clubs and charities. But whoever she chooses to bring home and introduce to her father would have his work cut out for him. Thankfully, that wasn't for a few years to come.

"What do you think about the color system I developed for the bows? The cookies going to the children's hospital are red and the ones for the nursing home are green," she said.

"Impressive and very organized. Emmie, how do you come up with these ideas?"

She shrugged her shoulders.

"I don't know. I just think of it and then make a plan."

"You make it sound so easy. Not everyone is as organized as you are. I could use that kind of organized thinking and creativity at the store. You may have to come and hang out with me for a couple of days while you're on Christmas break."

"Ooh, can I? That would be so cool. I could be your assistant and learn what it would be like to own my own business someday."

"I'd love to have you come to the store."

"Awesome. Maybe I can work with Natalie on a few projects."

"Oh, sweetheart, Natalie won't be there this time. She had to take some time off to be with her family."

"Oh," she said.

"Hey, you never told me you want to own a business someday. You've had the best teacher to learn from all these years. Your dad is the best business owner, you know."

"Yeah, but it's not the same. Dad does a lot of construction and I have no interest in that."

"Okay. Well, what do you have an interest in?"

"I want to have my own jewelry or clothing store someday. Hey, maybe it could be a clothing store with a jewelry counter. I can sell all the latest fashion for girls my age and older."

"It sounds like a lovely idea."

Cole walked in with his duffle bag in hand. He had such an unconventional sense of style. As long as he could throw a ton of work related items in it, he didn't care what it looked like.

"There's my two girls."

He removed flour from my nose and gave me a kiss.

"What do we have going on in the kitchen here? Let's see, cookies, bows, and a ton of sprinkles... looks like it has Emmie's name written all over it."

She giggled.

"It sure does. The master baker is at it again," I said.

"Let me guess. Is it for the nursing home this year? Or have you picked another group to donate to?"

"The cookies are for the nursing home and children who have to be in the hospital for Christmas."

"That's sweet, Emms. Where would the people of Pelican Beach be without you? Speaking of Pelican Beach, while I have the two of you here, I thought of a new Christmas Eve tradition that we could start this year. If you have a minute, I'd love to hear what you think about it."

"I'm all ears."

"Why don't we check out the new Festival of Lights this year? I heard it's going to be a spectacular show, with a guest appearance from Santa."

Emmie sighed.

"I get it Emmie, your way too old for Santa. However, you're never too old to enjoy a Christmas light show and grab a bite to eat afterward."

"If you want to throw in milkshakes after dinner, that would be a nice bonus."

"You drive a hard bargain, kiddo, but I think we can work something out. Payton, what do you say?"

"I think it's a great idea. It can be our own special little Christmas activity before the big day with the family. And to make it extra fun, when we get home, how about we open at least one gift?"

"Spoken like a true genius, but there's only one problem," Emmie said.

"What's that?"

"Dad told me the other day he was starting a 'no opening gifts before Christmas policy'."

I glanced over at Cole. He hadn't said a word about it to me. But, the big grin on his face revealed that he wasn't terribly concerned about enforcing the new policy.

"Emmie, I was just teasing. I think we can squeeze in one gift on Christmas Eve."

She pumped her fists in the air. "Yess!"

"Alright, the plans are in place and all that's left to do is deliver Christmas cookies first thing in the morning."

"Do we have time to stop by Grandma Helen's house after we drop off the cookies? I told her I would help with baking the desserts."

"That might be a little tricky because I have a doctor's appointment tomorrow at ten. Maybe Dad can help us out."

"I'm home for the next several days. I don't see why we can't make it a family affair. Let's drop off the cookies, hang with you for the appointment, and then stop by Helen's after," Cole said.

"Oh, I wouldn't want to drag you two along to the doctor's office. You'll be bored out of your mind."

"Nonsense, Emmie and I can entertain ourselves while we wait. Besides, I'm curious to hear what the doctor has to say, anyway. I was thinking how strange it is that whatever you have, neither of us have caught it. We're around each other all the time. It doesn't make sense."

"Maybe I need to work on my immune system, I don't know. Either way, I really can give you an update when I get back, Cole. After the appointment, I have to rush over to the store. With Natalie gone, I'll need to get there as quickly as possible to make sure the doors are open for customers until at least five o'clock. Long story, I'll catch you up to speed later, but basically she had to take off early to be with the family."

I gave Cole a look to signal that I would talk to him about it later. I don't know what was worse, the pressure of knowing that I had a hectic day to look forward to on Christmas Eve, or the pressure of not telling Cole the real reason for me scheduling the doctor's appointment. My gut was telling me it was the latter. Ultimately, I still really believed that I just had a week long stomach thing. Eventually it would go away. But, after getting such a bizarre reading on the pregnancy test, I didn't think it would hurt to ask the doctor to give me an official test to be sure. The lady taking my appointment didn't need to know all the details. I could casually mention it. After sharing my past history, they'd probably rule out pregnancy, anyway.

Around eight o'clock the next morning I was still wandering around in my flannel pajamas wishing I could go back to bed. The aroma from the freshly baked cookies made me want to hide in the bathroom, but I knew I had to push through it and put on a smile for Emmie. I splashed my face with cold water, patted it dry, and looked up in the mirror to see Cole standing in the doorway.

"You almost scared the daylights out of me. Make some noise the next time or something."

He laughed.

"I'm sorry, I thought you heard me."

The smell of the cookies grew stronger as he stood with the door ajar.

"Come on in and close the door."

"Uh, sure. You realize that Emmie is awake, right?"

"I'm not inviting you in here for alone time. I can't take the smell of the cookies and you're standing there with the door wide open."

"Oh, I'm sorry. Let me get the door for you. Payton, this is exactly what I was talking about last night. You have not been feeling like yourself for a while. If you can't bear the smell of cookies something is wrong. You need to see the doctor like pronto. I'm taking you to the appointment this morning and I'm not taking no for an answer."

"Cole, I'll be fine, I promise."

"I'm still not taking no for an answer. And, can we talk about why you've been so resistant lately? Is there something you don't want me to know?"

"No."

I waited another moment.

"Maybe," I said.

Cole took a seat on the edge of the bathtub and waited in silence.

"It's not that I don't want you to know. I just don't have anything to tell you at the moment. Other than, I took a pregnancy test with Abby, because I was wondering if I was..."

He leaped up faster than I could get the words out of my mouth.

"Pregnant?" Cole finished my sentence.

"See, that's what I was afraid of. I didn't want to get you all excited if it's nothing. I honestly don't believe there's a chance. But once Abby planted the thought in my head, I couldn't shake it loose."

"Well, what did the test say?"

"I think it was negative, but there was a faint plus sign that was appearing so it kind of freaked me out a little."

Cole removed the washcloth out of my hand and held me.

"Payton. All that matters to me is you get checked out to make sure you're okay. I'm already complete with you and Emmie, no matter what the result is."

"Thank you, babe. In that case, I'll gladly accept your invitation to escort me to the doctor's office....and to the store after....and to my mother's house...and you can help with the green bean casserole I plan to bring tomorrow as well."

"Whoa. Slow your horses. Let's start with Emmie and I dropping off the cookies and then swinging back around the house to pick you up. We may also want to take a raincheck on the Christmas lights for this evening."

"Let's see how I feel first. A change of scenery might do me some good."

Cole opened the door again and turned around to blow a kiss.

"Payton, you know you can always talk to me about anything, right?" he asked.

"Yes."

"Good, so promise me the next time something is bothering that pretty little head of yours you'll..."

"Cole!"

"Yes, honey."

"I love you. I really do. But, if you don't hurry up and close that door!"

He closed the door quickly, but on the other side I could hear him chuckling away.

"Payton, have you ever heard the old saying 'if it looks like a duck, swims like a duck, and quacks like a duck, then it's probably a duck'?"

"Yes, but what does that have to do with anything?"

"Based on the way you're acting, we might just have a little duckling in the making. I'm just saying."

"Cole Miller!"

"I love youuuuuu."

His voice faded off into the distance and I proceeded to slowly continue getting ready for the day.

HELEN

"*J*olene, we need to come up with a plan. I refuse to have chaos in my kitchen tomorrow just because you want to have a food contest. We need to stick to a solid schedule of who's going to be in the kitchen at what time."

"Well, good morning, to you, too, Scrooge."

"I'm being serious. The grandkids are going to be here later on to help with the baking, and the rest of the food needs to be in the oven bright and early tomorrow morning. That barely leaves time for you to make your rum cake and whatever else you had in mind."

"Helen, don't worry about me. I function at my best during the midnight hour. By the time you wake up on Christmas morning, I will have already prepared a feast to die for. And, I'll still have time left over to freshen up and look nice before my guest arrives."

"What guest?"

"Wouldn't you like to know?"

"Actually, I would. You didn't mention anything to me. Surely, it has to be someone from back home. You barely know anybody around here."

"I didn't mention anything because I just invited him the other day. Aren't you the one who always says the more the merrier?"

"Well, yes, but I'd still like to know who you picked up off the street to bring into my house, Jolene."

"There's no such thing as a stranger in Pelican Beach. And I didn't meet him in the street."

"Where did you meet him then?"

"At a local bar."

"You have to be kidding me. A bar?"

"Oh, Helen, it's not a big deal. I invited David, the new owner at the inn and his bartender, Frank, that's all. I'm not sure if Frank will come, but I know David is spending the holidays alone this year."

"Who?"

"The new owner at the inn you used to own. He seems like a nice guy and he's out here on his own with no family around, so I extended an invitation. Were you aware that he owns other inns in different states? I don't know how the man does it. I told him about making the place a little more... you know... small town friendly and less commercial. Other than that, things seem to be working out rather nicely at the inn."

"Jolene Ferguson, I could wring your neck. Why on God's green earth would you invite the new owner of our former business to our house? Of all places!"

"Why wouldn't I? You and Will have always been about hospitality. Plus, I thought it might be fun to hear him talk about how things are going. Maybe y'all could compare notes about your experiences. You know, chum it up about the business and whatnot."

Just listening to Jolene speak made my blood pressure rise. She was right back to stirring up trouble, and she did it so effortlessly. I was starting to think it was a natural part of her DNA.

"Take a deep breath, Helen. Don't lose it on her. Don't do it," I said out loud.

"Is it really that big of a deal? He'll be here for a couple of hours tops."

"Yes, it's a big deal. Payton and I weren't too fond of his way of doing business when he bought the inn. He came in with these grand ideas, including laying off the staff to bring in his own people. We sent him on his way the day he tried to sit down and negotiate an earlier closing date. He thought he could just throw a little extra cash around and have his way. I was fine with never seeing the likes of him again, and now you're bringing him to my house for Christmas."

"I didn't realize you had an issue with the guy. You and Will normally welcome everybody, no questions asked. If it's that big of a deal I'll go down to the inn and cancel our plans."

"You can't do that. You'll make the family look bad. I mean, what could you possibly say to him at this point? 'I'm sorry, but I need to take back your invite to dinner because the former owner doesn't really like you that much.'"

I took another deep breath.

"Look. What's done is done. Let's just welcome him in here for a couple of hours, like you said, and then he'll be on his way."

"You know, Helen, I spent some time talking with him and

he seems like a nice guy. He kind of reminds me of George with his mannerisms and all. Maybe it won't be as bad as you think."

"Jolene, he reminds you of George? Really?"

"A little," she murmured until her voice trailed off.

"He sure is handsome, I can tell you that."

"Ah, now the truth comes out. If I were you, I'd forget it. Don't even go there if you know what's best for you."

"Forget it? You must think I'm some old, shriveled up prune who doesn't notice a good-looking man when I see one."

"Honestly, I think just the opposite. I've seen how you look at men when we go out."

"What's that supposed to mean?"

I paused and looked at the clock on the wall. It was almost ten thirty on Christmas Eve and I was no closer to starting my baking than I had been before Jolene entered the kitchen.

The sooner I accepted this was who she was, the better off I'd be. I always felt like she dangled just enough bait to get me going and before I knew it I was in too deep. Not this time. Today, I was going to turn on my Christmas music and carry out my plans for dinner.

"It doesn't mean anything, Jolene. I think we should stop while we're ahead. I'm going to put on some music, put on my apron, and get to work in the kitchen. If you need me, you know where to find me."

The grandkids were scheduled to arrive in an hour. Will and I sat and ate lunch to the sound of rain slapping against the window pane. The views of the dark clouds moving across the water was enough to make me want to curl up with a blanket.

But, there was no time for that now. Instead, I spent a few minutes trying to get Will to indulge in small talk, just as I had done every day since his dementia diagnosis.

"What's the matter, Will? You don't feel like eating your pickles today?"

"No."

"Well, I better check your temperature and make sure you're feeling alright. You never skip out on your pickles and chips."

He stared past me looking out of the window, instead.

"It looks like we're going to have a wet Christmas this year. It's too bad. I know everyone in town was looking forward to seeing the Christmas lights tonight."

"Mmm hmm."

"You know, the grandkids will be here soon. I think I'll put Maggie and Emmie in charge of helping me with my cobbler and Aiden can decorate the cookies. I have this funny feeling he'll help out for a few minutes and then disappear on me. Maybe he can keep you company. I know you two love watching your sports."

"Yes." Will agreed.

"I have an idea. If you're feeling up to it maybe we can do something different tonight since it's Christmas Eve. Instead of going to bed early, maybe we can stay up and have some fun. Remember when you and I used to put the kids to bed and stay up in the living room all night long? One would've thought we were up wrapping gifts, but not us. We used to dance the night away to our favorite songs, like I'll Be Home for Christmas and Rockin' Around the Christmas Tree. Oh, boy, how I miss those days, Will, don't you?"

Again Will nodded his head and continued to listen to me

babble. I didn't mind. The doctor told me it was a good idea to share fond memories from our past. As long as it was helpful, I'd continue to do whatever I could for Will.

The phone rang.

"Hello?"

"Hey, it's me, Rebecca."

"Well, there you are. It's nice that you finally decided to call your mother. I don't know whether to welcome you back or if you're still out of town, or what."

"I'm back. I've just been busy. I figured I'd check in to see if there's anything you want me to bring to dinner tomorrow."

"Not so fast. I can't imagine you being so busy that you don't have time to check in and say hello. How's my grand-baby? I haven't seen him in so long he may not recognize me anymore."

"Okay, Mom. Don't you think you're being a little dramatic? John William didn't forget you. He's just been spending some time with Ethan's parents before the holidays, that's all."

"I told you they're invited to dinner, but I guess you were too busy to mention it to them."

"I did, but they have plans. It's not a big deal, really. So, is there anything you want me to bring?"

"Payton is bringing her green bean casserole, and I think Abby is bringing another side dish. If you just pick up plenty of drinks for the kids that will be fine."

"Are you sure?"

"Yes, I'm sure."

"Okay, I'll see you tomorrow."

Rebecca hung up the phone before I could say another word. I wanted to ask her to come clean and be honest about whatever was bothering her. But, apparently, whatever grudge she was holding would have to wait until after Christmas.

"Will, I don't know about your youngest child. I know I gave birth to her, but she has a stubborn streak that could've only come from your side of the family."

Jolene walked in just in time to hear what I was saying to Will.

"I beg your pardon. We're not stubborn, are we, Will? We might be a little crazy, but we're not stubborn."

"Crazy is an understatement," I mumbled under my breath.

"Cousin Will, it's time for your afternoon nap. I have your chair all set up and your favorite station is on. Let me help you up from the table so we can get you squared away," Jolene said.

Will waved his hand at her to get out of his way. He may not have been a man of many words, but he liked his independence whenever possible.

"Alright, off you go then. I see the both of you woke up on the wrong side of the bed this morning." She followed him out of the kitchen.

I shifted my attention back to the window that Will was staring out of. I could easily envision the younger version of ourselves running around in flip-flops and decorating the back porch with white lights everywhere. Our first Christmas at the cottage was a dream come true. Abby and Payton were knee high to a duck, and Rebecca was on the way. Now look at us. Our kids are all grown but we're still upholding family traditions that are rooted in love.

ALICE

"*D*on't get up yet. Let's lay here for five more minutes and listen to the sound of the rain." Stanley nestled close to me. He always made it difficult to part ways and step out of bed.

"Your bad habits are rubbing off on me, Stanley. Before we were married I used to get out of the bed no later than six-thirty. Now, look at me. It's almost seven o'clock and we have a lot to do before we head over to Helen's house later."

"Like what? All we have to do is make a light breakfast, eat it, and get dressed. I can do all that within an hour."

"You can, but I need extra time if I'm going to get this hair of mine to behave. Especially since it's raining."

I laid there a little longer to appease him. Stanley was highly skilled at sleeping through the night, waking up to pay his water bill, and going back to sleep again. I didn't know how he did it.

My body never allowed me to sleep past a certain hour, even when I was tired.

"Hey, Stanley."

"Yes, dear."

"Do you miss your old life?"

"Is this a trick question, Alice?"

"Ha. No, it's not a trick. I'm just curious. I always hear you reference what things were like before we were together. It made me wonder if you miss those times, that's all."

"No, I wouldn't trade my current life with you for anything in the world, Alice."

"Good answer."

"It's the truth! Yeah, sure, it was nice to toss my socks wherever they landed and not think about the consequences. But, that does nothing to cure a lonely heart."

"You never spoke about being lonely when we were friends."

"There was a lot I didn't talk about, but that doesn't mean it didn't exist. When you and I became friends, I grew accustomed to coming over and visiting you once a week. During the weeks we didn't see each other, I always missed you. That's how I knew I was falling for you."

"Well, if you're trying to win extra brownie points with me this morning, you're doing a good job."

We continued staring at the ceiling while talking. It seemed like the longer we laid there, the harder the raindrops began beating on the shingles.

"I'll bet everyone is moving just as slow as we are this morning with all that rain. Except the kids, of course. Emmie was probably up before daybreak just to see what was under the tree."

I laughed to myself.

"Emmie outgrew the idea of Santa Claus being real at an early age. But, that sure didn't stop her from waking up early to see what was under the tree. I used to spend the night on Christmas Eve just so I could be there to see her reaction to all the gifts she received."

"I'll bet. Alice, I guess I could ask you the same question you asked me. Do you miss your old life? I'm sure it must've felt different waking up without seeing Emmie on Christmas morning."

"Yes, and no. I'll always miss the extra time we had together. If you think about it, I had to step up and help big time when Cole's wife, Laura, passed away. Emmie needed me, and I was happy to be there for her. But, I also knew the importance of Cole getting back out there and falling in love again. So, I'm at peace. This is the way it should've been all along if Laura hadn't been taken away from us so suddenly. Now, that Payton is in our lives, she couldn't be more of a perfect fit for Cole and Emmie. I'm happy for them. I really am. And, I'm happy that I get to share my life with you."

"That makes me feel good to hear. I can think of a way you can show your appreciation."

I swatted him with one of my pillows.

"Stanley, don't you start. Let's get up now before we get into trouble."

"You know I don't mind getting in trouble with you."

"Stanley!"

"Alright, alright. I'm getting up now."

"How do you want your eggs this morning?"

"The usual."

"Scrambled with a side of ketchup. I'm on it. Oh, and, Stanley, one more thing."

"What's that?"

"Merry Christmas, love."

"Merry Christmas."

I'll bet if my late husband, Paul, was looking down on me from heaven, he'd be very happy for me. He always used to say that we weren't created to live life alone. Funny thing, when I met him, I never thought I'd get married. That was until I fell head over heals in love. My, how things have changed over the years. I'm no longer the young and vibrant teenager running around with a ponytail tied in a ribbon. My reflection in the mirror reveals more wrinkles and lines than ever. But on the inside, the desire to love and be loved is just as alive and vibrant as ever.

"Alice, the car is all packed up. The gifts are in the trunk, and your dessert is on the back seat. We have a forty-minute drive ahead of us. We better get on the good foot so we're not late."

"Okay, but before we leave, how do I look?"

"Absolutely terrible, now get in the car and let's go." He chuckled.

"Stanley, you're no help at all."

"You know I think you look stunning no matter what you put on. I never understand why you ask me those kinds of questions."

"I like to hear your opinion, that's why."

I glanced over at the back window of my little crossover, which was filled to maximum capacity. All I needed was a reindeer's nose on the hood and antlers sticking out the windows, and the look would've been complete.

"We should've called Cole and asked if he and Payton wanted to ride with us. We could easily scoop them up along the way," Stanley said.

"And where do you suppose they would fit? We barely have any room left in the car. Besides, I spoke to Cole briefly, and he said Payton was still feeling under the weather but starting to come around. I think they were buying themselves a little extra time before heading to Helen's house."

"Is Payton still sick? She wasn't feeling well the last time we were over their house. If you ask me, it's time she pays her doctor a visit."

"Mmm hmm."

"Would you care to explain?"

"Explain what?"

"What does 'Mmm hmm' mean?"

"It means I'll bet money Payton is pregnant."

"Do you think?"

Stanley pulled on the interstate and drove right into a sea of red brake lights.

"Here we go. A whole bunch of hurrying up only to stand still in traffic. Thankfully, we only have to endure this for two exits and then we can take the back roads out to Pelican Beach."

The wipers cleared off the remaining beads of rain on the windshield. In the distance there was a small glimpse of sunshine starting to break through with the darker storm clouds behind us.

"So what's this about Payton being pregnant?" he asked.

"I don't know it for certain, but I'm hearing all the tell-tale signs. I'd place a friendly bet with you in a heartbeat."

"If she is, how about I cook you dinner for a week?"

"Stanley, are you trying to give me food poisoning? I think I'll pass."

"Ha ha, I don't blame you. We'll have to come up with something else then. All jokes aside, I think it would be wonderful if they had a baby, don't you? Emmie would be such a good big sister."

"She would but I don't want to jinx it. Let's just wait and see. Whatever you do don't say a word. It's just a feeling I have in my gut, that's all."

"Mum's the word. Hey, Alice, can you do me a favor and reach for the pile of mail on the back seat? I was in a hurry yesterday and completely forgot I threw it back there. I think I saw a card from my brother Daniel if I'm not mistaken."

"Sure, let's see, we have value coupons, a real estate post card, and yep, a card from Daniel. Isn't that sweet that he sent you a card? You two really ought to stay in touch more. It's not like we're getting any younger, Stanley."

"I feel like it's my fault. Somehow I let the miles and my quiet nature get between us. Open up the card for me and see what it says."

We were still inching along with a half a mile left to our exit. I opened the card and showed Stanley the cover.

"Big Brother, it's been a while since we've seen each other. I hope this card finds you and your bride well. I'm happy you two found each other. I would love to plan a visit to come see you soon. We have a lot of catching up to do. Merry Christmas. Love, Daniel."

"That's nice. I'll have to call him and arrange something soon."

"We have plenty of space. Tell him he can come and stay at the house with us any time."

"Will do. Remind me to call him before we ring in the new year. For now, I think we're about to catch a break with this traffic. Let's get to Helen and William's house sometime before Christmas is over."

"Sounds good to me."

PAYTON

"Cole, I think we may have created a monster by getting Emmie a new cell phone for Christmas. She's already set up all her social media and now she's taking selfies for her profile pictures."

"I'm sure the newness will wear off after a while. I already told her the parental restrictions are coming down the pipeline, including turning the phone in at night before bed," Cole said.

"Poor thing. You know I'm just teasing about the monster part. Emmie's always been such a good kid. I'm sure she'll comply with the rules without a problem. I just hoped to see her open some of her other gifts before we leave for my parents' house, that's all. Speaking of my parents, what are your thoughts about us sharing the news with everyone at dinner?"

Cole was buried in his closet but managed to pop his head out to respond.

"Isn't there some kind of rule about waiting before you tell other people?"

"Typically, but we already told Emmie."

"Yeah, but that was kind of hard to avoid. She was hanging out in the waiting area at the doctor's office and there was no way we could endure a whole car ride in silence after finding out the big news."

"It was hard to contain myself yesterday. But what makes you think today will be any different? What am I supposed to say when everybody digs into dinner and I barely eat anything?"

"Maybe you'll have more of an appetite later on."

I just stood there and stared at Cole.

"Okay, maybe that won't work. Last night all I had to do was heat a plate of food and you were practically running to the bathroom at the smell."

"Exactly. Besides, do we really expect Emmie to keep such a big secret from the family? Your mother already looked suspicious the last time she was here. If I make up a story and tell everyone I still have a stomach bug, no one is going to buy into it. I'm still in total shock and disbelief, to be honest. When the doctor told us we were expecting, the news hit me like a ton of bricks. Good bricks, of course, but wow!"

"You looked as if you had seen a ghost." Cole laughed.

"I'll bet. It's so surreal, I still don't know what to make of it all. And, the look on Emmie's face when we told her was priceless. One would've thought she was about to become a mother."

I slipped on my leather riding boots over my jeans. At least now it made more sense why my jeans were feeling snug. We weren't big on formal attire for the holidays, so simple jeans and a cute top would do. I never understood why some of us Floridian women wore boots in the winter. It's not like we were expecting a heap of snow outside. Regardless, I still joined the masses and gave in to the latest fashion with one caveat. I always had a spare pair of flip-flops in my purse, just in case.

"Emmie is excited for sure. This morning she asked if I thought you would be okay with taking pictures of your belly on her cell phone. This way she could document your growth. I told her she needed to check with you on that one."

"Does she plan on posting the pictures online when I start looking like a great enormous whale?"

"Something like it."

I took a swing at him, but he grabbed me by the waistline and kissed my belly.

"I fully support whatever you decide. If you want to tell the family we're expecting, I'm all for it. If you want to wait, I'm for that, too. I'm so happy to be a dad again, I could scream it from a mountaintop. I love you, Payton."

"You always know how to make me smile, Cole. How about we play it by ear? If it feels right, then we'll share."

"I'll follow your lead."

He kissed me one more time before returning to his closet to rummage around. Cole was organized with most things in life, but his closet always looked like it was under an invasion or attack. I, on the other hand, amid all the joy, had something weighing on my heart that I needed to take care of.

"Can we be ready to leave in let's say, fifteen minutes?"

"I can be ready in less than fifteen if you need me to," Cole responded.

"No, fifteen is fine. I want to make an important call to wish a special someone a Merry Christmas."

"Okay, I'll be downstairs in fifteen," Cole said.

In the hallway, I glanced over the banister to see that

Emmie was dressed, ready to go, and still fully consumed by her phone.

"Emmie, give your eyes a break, love. I'm going to make a quick phone call and then we're going to head out, okay?"

"Okay."

I sat in the home office, took a deep breath, and dialed Natalie's number. I was uncertain whether anyone would answer, and a little nervous about what to say. Were there ever really any words of comfort to offer at a time like this? Christmas was supposed to be a joyous time, yet Natalie had such a heavy burden tugging on her heart with her mother's passing.

"Hello."

"Hi, Natalie, it's Payton."

"This is Natalie's aunt. Hold on a moment, I'll go get her."

They sounded so much alike it caught me off guard. I don't remember Natalie talking about her aunt much, but she was always rather private to begin with.

"Hi, Payton."

"Natalie, how are you?"

"I'm okay, I guess."

We sat in silence for a moment before I continued.

"I can't pretend to know what to say, Natalie. My intention was to wish you a Merry Christmas, but somehow those words don't seem appropriate for a time like this. I just know that it was on my heart to call and check on you and to let you know that I'm thinking about you."

"Thank you, Payton. I appreciate you calling. As my aunt reminded me, Christmas was my mother's favorite time of the year. If there's anything I know, Momma wouldn't want us to skip out on celebrating her favorite holiday. I know for certain she'd frown upon it. Even through the tears, I'll gladly accept your well wishes for a Merry Christmas, Payton. Mom wouldn't have it any other way."

"Natalie, you're one of a kind. I know your mother is looking down on you and is so proud of the wonderful young lady she raised."

"I hope so."

"Oh, I know so. The offer still stands to call me if you need help with anything. I'm here for you if you need me."

"I will. Enjoy your family dinner. Merry Christmas, Payton."

"Thank you and Merry Christmas to you, Natalie."

The cars were lined down the driveway at my parents' house. That's just the way Mom liked it. A house filled with family and laughter made for a merry occasion, no matter what time of the year it was. Their beautiful tree sparkled in the front window. I know Cole and I agreed to play it by ear, but just having everyone gathered together was enough to spark excitement about making our big announcement.

With all three of our hands weighed down with gift bags, Emmie wiggled a finger loose to ring the doorbell.

"Merry Christmas! Ho! Ho! Ho!" Wyatt answered with his Santa hat on.

"Merry Christmas, buddy. Long time, no see. Where's the rest of your suit?" Cole said.

"Man, it's almost seventy-five degrees and we have a house full of kids who are way past the Santa thing. All except for

Aiden, but I think he'll live. Come on in, guys. Let me help you with these bags."

"Merry Christmas, Wyatt." Emmie and I exchanged hugs with Wyatt before laying our things down and settling in.

Mom greeted us with her arms wide open.

"There you are. I was starting to wonder what was taking you so long. Abby, Rebecca, and the guys are all in the living room. Sweet Emmie, the kids started a game of volleyball in the backyard if you want to join them."

"Okay. Merry Christmas!" Emmie kissed Mom on the cheek and took off like something was after her.

"Payton, your skin looks absolutely radiant. Are you using a new beauty regiment? If so, I need you to share whatever your secret is with me."

"I'm not doing anything besides putting on extra layers to hide the circles under my eyes."

"Lack of sleep will do that to you," Cole said.

The minute the words slipped out of his mouth, he looked as if he regretted it.

"Why aren't you sleeping, Payton?" Mom asked.

"I don't know. It's probably exhaustion to be honest. The last couple of weeks have been a balancing act between the store, Christmas shopping, gift wrapping, you name it."

"Well, as long as you're taking care of yourself. That's what's most important. All the other things can wait," she said.

"What's that smell? I was expecting the usual aroma from your famous cooking to hit me when Wyatt opened the door. It smells different this year. Almost like a barbecue or something."

"Don't remind me. Jolene cooked a few dishes of her own. I'm not supposed to say anything. As if you wouldn't notice. All

I can say is proceed with caution. Maybe even have a bottle of anti-acid on hand just in case."

"Helen. It can't be that bad," Cole said.

"Alright. Don't say I didn't warn you."

"Well, I brought the green bean casserole. I'll let it sit in the oven until it's ready to be served."

"Good luck finding any room in the oven. She completely invaded my kitchen, and God only knows what she has roasting in the oven now. We had an agreement that she'd be done by the time I woke up this morning. Clearly that didn't work out."

The doorbell rang.

"You two go ahead and make yourselves comfortable. I'll get the front door."

In the living room, Ethan had everyone fully engaged in a game of Charades. It seemed to be our family "go to" game every time we gathered. Mainly because we could act silly and laugh over just how ridiculous everyone looked. The moment we stepped in the living room everyone pointed above our heads and cheered us on to kiss under the mistletoe. It was a new addition to my parents' Christmas decorations this year.

"Plant a big one on her, Cole!" Ethan yelled.

Cole and I kissed, feeling somewhat silly with such a big audience watching.

Jolene was highly amused by it all. "Ahh, so you like the mistletoe idea. Looks like you needed me around to spice things up around here. Don't worry, there's more where that came from," she said.

"That's what worries me most," Abby announced.

"Come here and give your big sister a hug," Abby said.

Afterward, Cole disappeared into the living room to talk to Wyatt and my dad.

"Payton, I've been meaning to ask you about the other day. Did you take another test or go to the doctor?" Abby whispered.

"I scheduled a doctor's appointment," I said. It was the first thing that came to mind.

"There they are. The Bobbsey Twins are at it again. You haven't been together for five minutes and you're already whispering and sharing secrets among one another." Rebecca interrupted.

"And Merry Christmas to you, too, Rebecca. Please tell me the evening isn't going to be filled with another one of your 'nobody pays me any attention' episodes," I said.

"I'm not sure what that's supposed to mean, Payton. All I know is I was coming over to wish you a Merry Christmas, but as usual, you and Abby are doing your own thing."

"We're not doing our own thing, Rebecca." Abby tried to convince Rebecca but her words fell on deaf ears.

"Never-mind, it's no big deal. I'm going to check on John William. It's time for him to wake up from his nap."

Rebecca walked off with a chip on her shoulder, which had become the norm for her these days. It amazed me that even on Christmas she couldn't lay her selfishness aside for just a little while, so everyone could enjoy themselves.

I turned to Abby.

"We need to have a sit down with her once and for all."

"She's all yours, Payton. I have enough on my plate to deal with. I love Rebecca, but she has a severe case of spoiled brat syndrome, and I have zero tolerance for dealing with that right now."

"She's not a child anymore, Abby. If you have an issue about something, the proper way to deal with it as an adult is talk it out."

"Payton, unfortunately some people never grow up. Our sister just might be one of those people."

Just then Mom announced Helen and Stanley's arrival.

"Look who's here, everybody."

Cole's face lit up the room at the sight of his mother's arrival. Not only was this our first Christmas as a married couple, but it was the first time we gathered all the family under one roof for the same holiday in a while. I brought my camera along to capture every moment from beginning to end.

While Cole went over to say hi to his parents, I snuck over to see my dad.

"Merry Christmas, Dad." I pulled up a chair next to his favorite recliner.

"Merry Christmas." He repeated.

"I see you and Cousin Jolene are keeping each other company over a glass of eggnog."

"That's right. What's Christmas without a little nog." Cousin Jolene interrupted.

"Did you spike the eggnog? You know Dad can't drink anything that's going to interfere with his medication."

"Payton, I worked as a nurse for over thirty years. I was a pretty darn good one, if I may say so myself. I have all the awards and accolades to prove it. Do you think I would give your father something he's not supposed to have?"

"I was just checking, that's all."

"Mmm. If it will make you feel better, sniff the glass. It's one hundred percent eggnog. Now, my glass on the other hand is mixed with the good stuff. I plan on having a good time tonight."

Again, the doorbell rang.

"And here comes my idea of a good time, right now. If you'll excuse me, I'm going to answer the front door. Payton, you should help yourself to a glass. Loosen up a bit, honey."

When Jolene was out of sight I jokingly pleaded with my father, hoping I could get him to give me some feedback about Jolene.

"Daddy, I know you, you don't like to make a fuss, but it's okay for you to admit if you're ready for Jolene to go back to Jacksonville. I wouldn't blame you one bit. That woman is as crazy as they come."

My dad didn't say much, but he smirked.

"Payton, do you have a minute?" Mom bent over to whisper.

"Sure, what's up?"

"I probably should've called you ahead of time to give you a heads up."

"About what?"

Jolene walked into the living room just as Mom was speaking. A gentleman was standing behind her with a cowboy hat on. As soon as he removed his hat, I had to do a double take just to make sure I was seeing right. I wondered why David Stonewall was standing in my parents' living room. Had Cousin Jolene invited him to dinner?

"Are my eyes deceiving me?"

"No, your eyes are working just fine. That's what I wanted to talk to you about. She's been spending time over at the inn and apparently she made a new friend."

"Okay, I'm all for making friends in the community. We've even been over to the inn to have dinner since we sold it, but he's the last person I'd expected to see at the dinner table today."

"Tell me about it. Jolene said that he's spending the holidays alone, so she invited him over. We'll just put on a smile and deal with it for a couple of hours, that's all. I already gave the others the heads up."

"Merry Christmas, everyone!" David nodded his head and held up a bottle of wine.

"I brought a few bottles of holiday cheer as a thank you for having me. Who here likes wine?"

Ethan and Wyatt gladly went over and shook his hand and welcomed him. Cole gave me a look of confusion from across the room, to which I just shrugged my shoulders in response.

～

The fixings were all set on the dining table and the final touches looked picture worthy. Mom extended the leaves to her farm-style table and placed several decorated mini tables around the room for the desserts. I don't know how she managed to pull off such a grand display, but she did. Before sitting down to say grace, we all posed for a family photo.

"Alright, everybody grab the hand of the person sitting next to you. Wyatt, if it's okay, I'd like to pass you the torch and give you the task of saying grace."

"Sure, everybody, please bow your heads. Heavenly Father, we thank you for blessing us with the meal before us, those that prepared the meal, and with every person seated around this table. May the love and blessings you share with us continue to surround us all this Christmas and through the New Year. Amen."

"Amen! Dig in everybody." Mom couldn't be more thrilled.

"Eh em. I'd like to say a few words while everyone fills up

their plate. I'm sure you all noticed some non-traditional items on the table this year."

"I thought we weren't going to say anything, Jolene." Mom interrupted.

"Helen, hush for a moment. I think you'll be pleased with what I'm about to say."

Mom sat back in her chair and pouted as if she had been scolded.

"Anyway. I was about to say that Helen was gracious enough to allow me to share some of my traditions as well. Most of you know that George and I were as non-traditional as they come. Therefore, there was nothing abnormal about having a spaghetti dinner, or pulled pork with barbecue sauce, as long as we were together and happy. I initially challenged Helen to a cook off. But, seeing how tradition is so important to you all, I thought better of it. If you're willing to try my food, enjoy it. If not, I'll understand that, too. Merry Christmas, everybody!"

"Cheers! Thank you, Jolene. And, Merry Christmas. Now can we eat?" Mom said.

"You don't have to ask me twice. Dig in!"

"Good. Okay, everybody, over here we have my famous apple and cranberry dressing, your grandma's cabbage recipe, oh and don't forget about the corn pudding. And, let's not forget, Jolene's Texas barbecue. To my surprise, it truly is to die for!"

"To your surprise? Helen, I told you I can cook!"

Everyone ate and passed around the serving dishes to one another. For a tiny moment in time it felt like we were a picture perfect family straight out of a scene from the Brady Bunch.

"Wow, Cousin Jolene and Mom are actually getting along for a change! I was starting to wonder if my eyes were deceiving me. It's like you've suddenly become two peas in a pod," Rebecca said.

I should've known whatever hopes of peace I envisioned for the day were about to dissipate as soon as Rebecca opened her mouth.

"Rebecca, of course we're getting along. It's Christmas. Mind your manners, sweetheart," Jolene said.

"Mind my manners? Hmm, that's an interesting comment to make. You weren't minding your manners the last time I was over here to visit." Rebecca picked up her glass of wine and took another huge gulp.

Somehow all the cheer and laughter started dwindling as everyone shifted their attention to Rebecca's end of the table.

"Rebecca, maybe you ought to lay off the wine for a little while," Mom said.

"It is the finest wine we have in stock. I figured I couldn't show up with the cheap stuff. Only the best for the Matthews!" David chuckled.

"Thank you, David. It's delicious. I'm on my third glass and I feel like I could have another. But could we all just sit back for a moment and address the pink elephant in the room? Surely I'm not the only one who sees it," Rebecca said.

"Rebecca!"

"No, Momma, please, allow me. We have David sitting here having Christmas dinner with us, which is fine and all." She turned and look at David.

"Nothing personal, David, I love the wine, keep it coming. Anyway, no one has explained how this came about. Last time I checked, he wasn't on Mom's list of favorites, and now here he is! Who's coming to dinner? Oh, just the new owner of the inn. You know, the guy who fired all the old staff and the guy who

Mom can't stand. And, as if that weren't enough, we have Mom and Jolene."

"That's Cousin Jolene to you," Jolene said.

"Excuse me. Mom and Cousin Jolene pretending to get along when the entire world knows you're usually at each others' throats. And, finally, you have my sisters who are walking around keeping secrets, as if they're the only ones who are privileged to know anything."

"Rebecca, that's enough. You've had too much to drink. Go upstairs and cool off."

"Looks like I'm not the only one who spiked their eggnog." Jolene snickered.

"I'm sorry, but I'm not going to be sent to my room like a little girl."

Ethan picked up John William, who was getting a little fussy at the table.

"I've been keeping everything bottled up inside long enough. The women are always putting on airs in this family, pretending to be oh so perfect, but that's just not the case. And, whenever I try to step in and help or simply be there for you, I'm the one who ends up getting chastised."

Alice and Stanley stopped eating. Abby and Wyatt had a slight frown on their faces while Rebecca continued to ramble.

"I know the real deal about each and every one of you, and unlike yourselves, I don't go around pretending. I'm a realist. I'll bet I can go around this table and tell you everything you've ever tried to keep from me starting with you, Miss goody two shoes, Payton."

I drew my head back in disbelief.

"Rebecca, I thought I asked you..." Mom started to reprimand her again but I wanted to hear more.

"Oh, no, Mom. Don't stop her now. I've had just about enough of Miss sassy pants over here. Let's hear what she has to say. Whatever it is, I'll bet there's no truth to it, anyway." I welcomed Rebecca's remarks.

"Why don't you just go ahead and tell everyone that you're pregnant and get it over with?"

"You little..." She was lucky there were children in our midst.

Everyone's expression turned to shock around the table, including Cole.

"You already told Rebecca that we're expecting?" he asked.

"No, babe, she only suspects that's the case because she walked in on Abby and I taking the test the other day. I never said a word to her or anyone else for that matter."

"Rebecca, how did you find out?" I asked.

"I've had my share of tests with mixed results. Plus, you just confirmed it by hardly putting anything on your plate. I've seen that nauseated look on your face before."

"That's pretty low, Rebecca."

She swallowed some more wine before continuing.

"Low? Low is what Mom did when I tried to defend her from Jolene's insults. Low is what Abby does every time she puts me down, like I'm a little child."

"That's because you are one. You're acting like one right now, even in front of our guests. You just can't seem to help yourself." Abby rolled her eyes.

"Rebecca, did it ever occur to you that I didn't need you to defend me from Jolene? I know how to defend myself. We were just two grown women having a minor disagreement. Do you think I didn't know what I was getting myself into when I asked her to come live with me? She was drunk as a skunk that night.

Who's to say there's any truth to anything she says when she's been drinking."

"Excuse me?" Jolene sat upright.

"Oh, Jolene, you know what I mean. How many times do you and I go at it and then forget about it the next day like it was nothing? It's happened so many times I've lost count."

As I looked around the table, Dad, Stanley, and the kids were the only ones still eating. Everyone else was too distracted by Rebecca's performance to finish their meal.

"Okay, here we go pretending again. We're just going to blame it all on Cousin Jolene who had way too much to drink and there's no truth to anything she said that night. Look out everybody, here comes the pink elephant again." Rebecca was in rare form.

"What on earth are you talking about?" Mom asked.

"Mom, whatever it is, now is not the time or the place. Clearly she's had too much. I don't see why we would sit here and listen to one more minute of this." I tried to intervene.

"Rebecca. I'm waiting. What are you referring to?" Mom said.

"Cousin Jolene referred to you having another love interest in your early days of being married to Dad."

The room fell silent, except for the kids who had just left the table.

Jolene leaned over and spoke in a low voice.

"David, pass me some more of that eggnog and brandy over there. It's going to be a long night."

Rebecca continued.

"I know she was telling the truth because I had a nice long conversation with John Murphy during my visit to Savannah.

You didn't want me to know the truth. That's why you hushed me up that night," she added.

As soon as the words came out of her mouth, I envisioned myself hurling the entire dish of green bean casserole right at Rebecca's face. Thankfully, Cole gripped my hand under the table. It was almost as if he could read my mind.

Mom slowly backed her chair away from the table and rose up. She looked angry enough to let Rebecca have it. Before she could speak we all heard a loud scratching sound coming from the record player in the living room. Dad managed to slip away from the table without being noticed. He gently put the needle down again and the sound of Elvis' I'll Be Home for Christmas filled the cottage. It was Mom and Dad's favorite Christmas song as young lovers. He returned to the dining table and extended his arm to mom for a dance.

Mom slowly began to light up with a smile, completely leaving behind all the words exchanged at the table.

"It's our favorite Christmas song. William Matthews, you never cease to amaze me. You remembered it all by yourself, darling. You remembered."

She laughed.

"You remembered!"

Mom cried tears of joy while slow dancing with Daddy. It was a big deal, if only for a moment, that he remembered something so near and dear to Mom's heart. It made us all a little teary-eyed. Abby and Wyatt joined my parents for a dance, and even Alice and Stanley nestled a little closer at the dinner table.

Rebecca slipped out of the room. I'm sure the embarrassment was more than she could bear.

Cole tapped me on the shoulder and spoke softly in my ear.

"I think there's room on the dance floor for two more, don't you?"

"I sure do. But first, Cole, I'm really sorry about the way things came out today. I promise I didn't say anything."

"I know, babe. Not to worry, let's join the family and have a good time. Besides, they still don't know the best part yet."

"Should we announce it now?" I asked.

"Why not? They all could use a little uplifting news right about now."

I giggled uncontrollably.

"You go ahead and announce it, Cole."

"Right now? Okay. Hey, everybody!" Everyone looked over at Cole.

"In effort to keep the good cheer going, Payton and I have some news to share." Cole looked at me and we both yelled together.

"We're having twins!"

Everyone cheered and joined us in a group hug. What could've been a terrible end to Christmas dinner turned out to be the best evening imaginable.

HELEN

"*P*ayton and Abby, whatever you don't eat I want you to take and share with everybody at home. There's plenty to go around. One of my favorite things about the day after Christmas is having you over to finish the rest of the food."

"I think everybody can agree the food always tastes better the second day. Besides, the worst is to enjoy a big feast at someone else's house and go back home to an empty fridge." Abby frowned.

"Same here. This morning Emmie woke up talking about Cousin Jolene's barbecue, and Cole wanted more cabbage," Payton said in between taking bites.

"There's plenty more where that came from. Isn't that right, Jolene?"

"Yes, ma'am. Take as much as you like. That way you can spare me from packaging and freezing everything."

"Payton, I'm so glad to see you have more of an appetite today. You didn't have much on your plate last night. The babies need their nutrition."

"Don't worry, Mom. I'm giving them as much as I can. I'm sure as soon as I get past this stage of sporadic nausea then everything will be just fine."

"I'm sure it will. Payton, I'm so happy for you and Cole. To think after all these years you didn't believe you could get pregnant. It just wasn't meant to be in your previous marriage. God has his perfect timing, and I'm so happy the time is now, with Cole."

"So am I. Although I will not lie. The doctor made me a little nervous with all the high-risk pregnancy talk because I'm over thirty-five. It's not exactly what you want to hear after finding out such good news."

"Payton, women do it all the time. You're not the first and you won't be the last, dear," I said.

"I know. Just tell that to my nervous system."

"You'll be fine, Payton, really. And you know we'll be there with you every step of the way," Abby said.

"You girls sure have stuck together like glue over the years, haven't you?" Cousin Jolene asked.

"Pretty much. This is the first time we're coming together the day after Christmas for lunch at Mom's house without Rebecca," Abby replied.

"Yeah, you're right. Even when I was married to Jack and living in Connecticut, I always managed to be here for Christmas week. I'm sorry to bring it up but have you spoken to her since last night, Mom?"

"No. Ethan quietly got her things together, packed the baby

up, said goodnight and they were on their way. I really think she had too much to drink. "

"Even if that's the case, it's still no excuse. She almost ruined Christmas for everybody. The least she could do is apologize. And, what about you, Cousin Jolene?" Payton seemed downright irritated. So was I for that matter.

"What about me? I didn't create a scene at the dinner table. My guest and I were on our best behavior."

We all looked at Jolene. Only she would think it was a good idea to bring the new owner of the inn to the house, creating such an awkward situation. It just so happens he was a younger looking version of her husband George, and when I say younger, I really mean a lot younger! I could see how she would be attracted to him. Especially after a few glasses of her favorite beverage. But what on earth he saw in her, I'll never understand.

"You were on your best behavior alright. I'm going to call you Cousin Jolene, the flirt."

"Abby, I do not understand why you would say such a thing." Jolene played innocent but we all knew better. She couldn't even keep a straight face because she knew Abby was telling the truth.

The doorbell rang.

"Mom, are you expecting company?" Payton asked.

"Not that I'm aware of."

"I'll bet five bucks it's Rebecca," Payton said.

"Don't even waste your money, you know how stubborn she is. It will be days before she comes around to admitting she was wrong," Abby said.

"Oh, come on. It's just a little friendly wager."

"Will you two stop it?" I said.

Sure enough, at the front door I could see Rebecca's silhouette through the side panel. Whatever she had come to say after yesterday's fiasco had better be really good. I opened the door and waited for her to speak. When she said nothing I turned around and started heading back to the kitchen.

"We're in the back having lunch if you'd like to join us. Close the door behind you."

Rebecca entered the kitchen with a shy and timid look on her face. I was having a hard time falling for it. There was nothing about my youngest child's fiery personality that was shy or timid.

"Grab yourself a plate," I offered.

"Thank you, but I didn't come to stay long. I figured you all would be here, and I just wanted to come by and apologize for my behavior last night."

Payton leaned over to Abby. "I would've totally won the bet," she said out loud.

"Uh oh, let me grab some popcorn for round two. This is better than my daytime soap operas. Much more entertaining," Jolene said.

Rebecca rolled her eyes at Jolene.

"My momma used to tell me if I rolled my eyes they would wind up permanently in the back of my head," Jolene said as she made a plate of food.

"Rebecca, have a seat." I motioned toward a chair.

She sat at the center island and began to speak.

"I owe all of you an apology for what I said last night. I had way too much to drink and completely embarrassed myself and all of you, of course."

"If that's how you behave after having a few of glasses of wine, then I'd hate to see what would happen if you had hard liquor." Jolene continued to tease.

"Jolene!"

"No, she's right. I already had a few glasses before we left the house. I anticipated it was going to be a difficult night and tried to do whatever I could to relax. Either way, there are no excuses to justify my actions. I'm sorry."

"Rebecca, why were you expecting anything other than just having a good time with your family? I don't get it. You've had this ongoing chip on your shoulder ever since we all drove out to the countryside to pick out a tree. And, the things you said last night were terrible. You ought to be ashamed of yourself. Don't think for one minute that it was a coincidence that your father turned on the record player at just the right time. I believe he did it to shine a light on what's most important. Our love that stood the test of time is what's most important. Not something that's been buried in the past and is no longer apart of our lives. No, ma'am. Both you and John Murphy lost this battle."

"Don't be mad at him, Mom. I'm the one who poked around and asked him questions."

"He should've referred you back to me. And, then there's Payton. Spoiling her announcement like that."

"I swear I didn't know. It was just a guess." Rebecca looked toward Payton and a tear ran down her face.

"I'm sorry, Payton."

"Hey, what about me? You weren't too nice to me either, young lady. I figured you were probably just jealous of me and my hot date," Jolene said.

Payton spit her soda out across the table. Leave it to Jolene to say something so ridiculous in the middle of a serious conversation. I was thankful for her just the same. We needed someone to break the tension. Although I was spit fire mad at Rebecca, she is my daughter and I knew eventually I'd come around to forgiving her. This time, at least.

"I'm sorry, I'll clean it up. Cousin Jolene caught me off guard. You really have the hots for David don't you, Jolene?" Payton asked.

"Nahh, that was my silly way of making y'all laugh. He's cute and all, but nobody can love me the way my George did. I was just trying to save this young lady from being disowned by her family, that's all."

"Nobody is going to be disowned," I said.

"Not this time. Let her try it again and you might sing a different tune." Jolene instigated.

"Jolene!"

"There won't be another time. I won't lie. I hate feeling like no one respects me in this family. I always get told to hush up, or I'm the last to know what's going on. It feels like everyone always keeps secrets from me and I can't stand it. But that doesn't give me the right to hurt you back. From the bottom of my heart, I'm truly sorry."

"Rebecca, I don't think anyone is intentionally trying to do anything to hurt you. But if you really want to be respected, it has to begin with you growing up and acting more mature. We're tired of having these interventions with you," Abby said.

"And, my darling daughter, if I might add one last thing. There's a big difference between someone keeping a secret from you versus you minding other folks' business. I love you with every fiber of my being, but what happened between your father and I is our business. We're the ones who get to decide if we want to share our story. Not the other way around."

"You're right, Mom. You're all right. I'm the one who's to blame."

"You're not entirely to blame. If I hadn't been rattling off at the mouth the night you came over, this probably wouldn't be a topic of conversation. I take responsibility for my wrongdoing as well." Jolene confessed.

Everybody sat in silence for a moment.

"Hey, it's rare that I apologize about anything so you better take it for what it's worth. They don't call me a pistol for nothing." Jolene chuckled.

"I second that, Jolene. But, since we're all gathered here, I'm going to put this topic to rest once and for all."

"Mom, you don't have to put anything to rest," Payton said.

"I know, but I want to. I don't want John Murphy to have the last word on what happened many years ago. I want to share my side of the story. When I look at Rebecca, I see a mirror image of myself over forty years ago. I was a free spirit, hot tempered, and even..."

"A party animal." Jolene interrupted.

"Yes, that, too. Even as a newlywed I had my share of having a good time until the sun came up."

"A few times we didn't know where we were the next morning when we woke up!" Jolene said.

"Jolene, this is my story. May I tell it please?"

"I'll hush. Go right ahead." She urged.

"We always had a good time while visiting your uncle. During the last summer festival we attended we should've been satisfied with the day's events and called it a night. But we didn't. There was always an after party with us. Unfortunately, too much drinking and partying never leads to anything good. After a night of backyard dancing and carrying on, John's brother, invited me to take a walk. We were all good friends, so why would I think anything of it. Plus, like yourself, Rebecca, I had more to drink than I should've. Jolene was there. She could tell you. One thing led to another and I found myself in his arms. He even went as far as kissing me before, thankfully, your father walked in and knocked the daylights out of him."

"That's it? This whole thing was about a kiss?" Rebecca asked.

"Rebecca, I was a married woman. I had no business wandering off with anybody except my husband."

"Okay, I get that. But, I'm sure John's brother knew what he was doing as well."

"It didn't matter. I had to take responsibility for my actions. Your father defended me, but I know I hurt him at his core. For a while I was afraid he wouldn't speak to me anymore."

"It's interesting you should say that, Helen. I figured William would be a little upset, but I was always confident that you'd continue to be together until the very end. Never once did I think you two would split after that happened. George felt the same way. I'm sure he'd say the same today if he were living. I know he would," Jolene said.

"Thank you, Jolene. It was still a terrible thing to go through. It embarrassed me among family and friends, and it created a wedge between Will and I for a little while. I vowed to him and myself that I would never go down that road again."

"It looks like we've all been through our trials," Abby said.

"Yes, but we're still here. Together and stronger than ever. That's what's most important. Not some mistake that happened over umpteen years ago," Payton added.

"Man, I really feel like a piece of dirt. I was being such a hot head. My feelings were hurt and I was just acting out of my emotions and not considering the cost. The truth is, if it weren't for you and Dad pressing through the most difficult times together, there would be no Abby, no Payton, or me. I wouldn't have a husband or a son to call my own. We wouldn't be a family."

"There she is. Ladies and gentleman, the level-headed side of Rebecca has finally resurfaced," Payton said.

"Shut up, Payton!" Rebecca giggled.

"I'm serious. I welcome this version of you to hang out and stay a while." Payton walked over and mashed the side of Rebecca's head on her shoulder.

"Yes, please do us all a favor and warn us before your evil twin returns. That girl is a force to be reckoned with. You can't tell her anything!" Abby ruffled up Rebecca's hair a bit just to mess with her.

"I promise to try to keep her at bay. But, seriously, you guys, I'm really sorry for all the drama yesterday and all the pain I caused. Mom, I'm your youngest, and I'm still learning. Please forgive me. And, Payton, again I'm so sorry to you and Cole. You deserved a spotlight on your special announcement and I took that away from you."

"Actually, you didn't take anything away from us. After you left, we announced that we're expecting twins," Payton said.

"What! Oh my gosh, I'm so excited for you!! Please let me make it up to you by throwing your baby shower!"

"Everybody standing in this room is my witness. On this day, December twenty-sixth, Rebecca is claiming full responsibility for throwing my baby shower!"

"Consider it done." Rebecca gave Payton a high five.

We settled our differences that day over leftover Christmas dinner and words of wisdom from Jolene. It reminded me that my family was everything but perfect. Not that I ever really thought we were the picture of perfection, but I did have a way of welcoming pink elephants in the room and being overly concerned about our image. It was time to let that go and cling even harder to what mattered most, family.

EPILOGUE: PAYTON

I t felt good to have the family back to some sense of normal after our Christmas fiasco. The new year was upon us and I was back in full swing at the store, with Abby as my temporary help. I received a call from Natalie requesting to take a leave of absence for a couple of months. She said she was going back to Texas with her aunt to clear her mind and decide on her next steps. I understood and wouldn't think of denying her the time. Although, I had a funny feeling she wouldn't be returning after announcing she was going to Texas. Only time would tell.

"Okay, Abby, spill it."

"What?"

"Whatever is bothering you, just spill it already. You haven't been acting like yourself for the last couple of days. It's like you have something weighing on your mind and you're in a daze."

"You know me too well, Payton."

"We've only been sisters for an entire lifetime. If I don't know you by now, then something is wrong. So, spill it. What's bothering you?"

"Wyatt and I are having financial problems. Major financial problems. And, of course, I wanted to put on a smile for the family over the holidays. But in reality, I'm distracted with thoughts of how we're going to get ourselves out of this mess."

"How bad is it?" I asked.

"It's to the point where I have to give up my dream of staying at home with the kids to help make ends meet. We have a ton of consumer debt that's been piling up. You know how it goes. A minor charge here, and a minor charge there. It all adds up. That plus the cars and the house. Something has to give."

"I'm sorry. I had no idea."

"Neither did I. Wyatt always takes care of the bills, and he's terrible when it comes to telling me no. When I wanted the neighborhood with all the nice amenities he said yes, when I wanted a new SUV he said yes, and even down to all of our shiny toys and gadgets. It was always a yes. It's not even fair for me to blame it all on him. It's my fault, too. Anyway, we're getting down to the wire and I'm applying for jobs as we speak. It's actually good that we're talking about this now, Payton. If I get a job offer, I'll have no choice but to accept, which means I won't be able to help at the store anymore."

"Abby, I think I have an idea. For now, would you consider working here at the store with me? I can guarantee you a full-time position for the next couple of months. Maybe you wouldn't have to worry about the job search until Natalie confirms her return date. What do think?"

"Really? That would be fantastic. But are you sure? I mean,

I'd put in the work, but are you sure you want to work with your sister?"

"Why not? It's a win-win situation if you ask me. I don't have to worry about being shorthanded, I totally trust you, and it buys you a little time to figure out your next steps. Plus, you can start getting paid!"

"Payton, I can't thank you enough. This truly means the world to me."

"Come here and give me a hug. You're always trying to be the tough older sister who can handle everything on her own. It's okay to let others look out for you sometimes, Abby."

"Ha, I'm learning that lesson now more than ever."

"Good. Now that I helped you solve your problem, I need help solving a problem that showed up in the mailbox yesterday."

"What's up?"

I laid an envelope down on the counter with the flap wide open. A handwritten letter was partially exposed, revealing cursive writing in blue ink.

"I didn't think people wrote letters anymore. Who's this from?"

"She goes by the name of Maxine."

"And? Who's Maxine?"

"I don't want to spoil it for you. First, read the letter for yourself, then we can talk about Maxine after."

"Okay."

Abby pulled the letter out and read it out loud.

"For starters this Maxine has beautiful penmanship."

I tapped my fingers on the counter, waiting for her to begin.

"Alright already. I'm reading."

'Dear, Payton. I should begin by introducing myself. My

name is Maxine Waters. You don't know me very well, but you were once married to my fiancé, Jack. I'm sure the last thing you would expect is to receive a letter from someone like myself, but I'm in quite a predicament and I could really use your help. I found your name on some old bills stored away in his files. That coupled with the fact that he shared that you moved back to Pelican Beach made it easy for me to look you up. Please don't be offended. I promise not to make a habit of contacting you often. The reason I'm writing is Jack and I are within ninety days of being married. However, to say he's struggling with his health and mental well-being would be an understatement. I accepted his proposal and vowed to be with him even through the toughest of times. However, recent concerns about Jack's past have surfaced and there are a lot of questions that Jack won't answer. I'm almost certain you can help fill in the gaps with questions regarding gambling and perhaps even questionable relation-ships. Again, I realize this may be a bit much to receive in a letter from a woman you don't know, but I'm in desperate search of the truth, and I have a decision to make within the next ninety days. Talking to you could be just what I need to help give me peace and put my mind at ease. Please consider reaching out to the number I've included below. If I don't hear from you, I'll understand that as well. Sincerely, Maxine.'

"Oh...my... goodness! Are you serious? Payton, I swear that meeting Jack was the worst thing that ever happened to you. It's like he never goes away. One way or another, he always squirms his way back into your life."

"Gee, thanks, Abby. You think I would've ever married him if I knew all the drama he would cause?"

"Of course not, but still. You have to admit this is getting to be over the top."

"You think? I showed it to Cole, and he about lost his mind. He already had me beef up the security cameras the last time Jack showed up at the store."

"So you told Cole? That's a good thing. I would imagine he's not a fan of you responding to this letter, right?"

"Right, and that makes two of us. I don't want to have anything to do with it. I felt sorry for the girl when I read it, but that's their situation and not mine. I have a family and two babies on the way, and my primary concern is safely delivering these babies with no issues along the way. That's it."

"Good. Keep it that way. Wow, this just goes to show you how jacked up his life was. No pun intended."

"You're such a goofball, Abby."

"Thanks!"

"Jack hasn't been on the straight and narrow for a long time. I'm questioning if I ever knew the real Jack or if it was all a facade."

"I don't know, Payton, but I say let the past stay right where it belongs. Where's your trash can?"

"Right over here."

"Good. Let's just place this bad boy in the circular file and move on with our lives. Now, on to better news," Abby said.

"Yes, please shower me with some good news."

"Remember on Christmas night when Dad played their favorite song on the record player?"

"Yes."

"Mom told me ever since then she's been playing some of their favorite songs, hoping it would jog his memory. Last night she stumbled on the song Dad played on the day he proposed.

When she played it, she said he lit up with a smile, and he kissed her ring finger. Payton, sometimes I really believe there's hope for him yet. I know what the doctors say, but I also know what I feel in my heart."

"Abby, that's amazing. We just have to remain hopeful and take things one day at a time. It's the same way Dad is dealing with it. One day at a time, right?"

"You're right."

Abby held her arms open wide.

"Where would we be without each other, Payton? Where would we be without our family?"

"I don't even want to consider the thought. I love you, Sis."

Abby poked my little baby bump. "And Aunty Abby loves you, too, baby beans."

Collectively, we all agreed on at least one resolution that year. It was to bury the things that served no purpose and invest in the hope of what lies ahead. We were all looking forward to what was on the horizon. Not just the new year itself, but for me, new life.

Ready to continue on to Book five, Sunrise At Pelican Beach? CLICK here or turn the page to learn more!

NEW BAHAMA BREEZE SERIES!

When Meg Carter advances a year's worth of rent on a beach house, she's shocked to land and discover it's been sold at an auction.

The new owner, Parker Wilson, is forty, a real estate investor, and ready to get the property flip underway.

When Meg digs her heels in and refuses to leave, will this drive them to become fierce enemies?

Or will they find common ground and potentially become sweet lovers?

Pull up your favorite beach chair and watch as Meg and Parker's story unfolds in this new Bahama Breeze Series today!

Tropical Breeze Series:
Tropical Encounter: Book 1
Tropical Escape: Book 2
Tropical Moonlight: Book 3
Tropical Summers: Book 4
Tropical Brides: Book 5

SOLOMONS ISLAND SERIES

Come visit us on Solomons Island. A beach
series with stories of heartwarming love,
friendships, and even a little drama in this
small-town saga.

With multiple love stories to follow, and a
community that sticks together, the cast of
characters on Solomons are sure to keep you
coming back for more!

Book one begins with Clara and Mike's love
story. So,
pull up a beach chair, your favorite beverage,
and fall in love with Solomons Island.

PELICAN BEACH SERIES

Pack your bags and enjoy beautiful sunsets at Pelican Beach! Like anywhere you may visit, there will be a little drama, and maybe even some unwanted competition. But the main dish being served in this series is love sweet love!

Pelican Beach Series:

The Inn at Pelican Beach: Book 1
Sunsets at Pelican Beach: Book 2
A Pelican Beach Affair: Book 3
Christmas at Pelican Beach: Book 4
Sunrise At Pelican Beach: Book 5

Made in the USA
Middletown, DE
17 November 2023

42843225R00093